ESCAPE

Part 1

SYDNEY
HOLMES

ESCAPE
Sydney Holmes

ESCAPE Copyright © 2014 SYDNEY HOLMES

Published by: Crespi House Publishing
ISBN: 978-1-941591-03-1 Print
ISBN: 978-1-941591-04-8 E-Book

www.SydneyHolmes.com

Formatting by Amy Atwell at Author EMS
Cover design by Karen Windsor-Worrel at KWW Design LLC
Edited by Bev Katz Rosenbaum at BKR Editing Services
and Valerie at Loud Lit Chicks

Published in the United States of America.

DEDICATION

To anyone who has fought to create a life they wanted
instead of succumbing to a predetermined destiny.
This book is for you.
Fight hard, your life is waiting for you.

BOOKS BY SYDNEY HOLMES

ESCAPE SERIES
Escape Part One
Escape Part Two
Escape Part Three
Escaping With Eve

AWAKENING SERIES
Awakening
Awake

Coming Soon

ESCAPE SERIES
Cody's Story
Rob's Story

ALYSSA MALONE MYSTERIES
Shoot The Moon
Paradise Awaits
Midnight's Breath
Red Skies At Night

CHAPTER ONE

Sweat dripped off her skin, sliding down her back. The rising heat made her head spin, but Rowan stood her ground ticking off the seconds. *Water*. She really needed more water, but now wasn't the time. The smell permeated her nostrils and burrowed into her brain. Never again. The smell of burning meat overwhelmed her brain and she knew she would never be able to eat beef again.

"Two more cheese burgers and a corn dog," Tami yelled in her direction.

Rowan nodded and watched as the burgers oozed their juices over the grill and the meat turned from soft pink to brown. The deep fryer to her left bubbled rapidly, sending yet more grease and heat into the air. Even wearing only a pair of shorts and a thin tank top, her face was hot. The thick apron somewhat protected her clothes from the grease and slime, but nothing could protect her from the stifling hot air.

"You get that, Rowan?" Tami asked.

Tami was one of the teenagers she supervised. For an extra buck fifty an hour, Rowan agreed to be the manager of the local pool's Snack Shack. The management had been thrilled to have a 31 year old apply for the position, and in the cool offices of the Community Center it seemed like a really good opportunity, but now, sweating like a pig and working the grill because none of the teenagers wanted to get greasy, she was seriously questioning that decision.

"Yeah, thanks Tami. Can you please check the fries? We don't want to run low on them," Rowan said, flipping the burgers and throwing two more on the grill. Reaching down to get the buns, she noticed they were out. She'd have to make one of the girls work the grill while she went to the stock room.

"Julie, after you start that corn dog, you need to cook these for me while I run to restock." Rowan called toward the other side of the tiny kitchen.

"Ohhhh, Rowie. Do I have to?" Julie whined.

Rowan wanted to slap her. Never in her life had she heard a sixteen year old whine so much. That would've never been tolerated back home. Hell, that would've never even happened. No one whined — ever.

"Julie, get an apron and don't burn these burgers. The lunch rush is just starting," she told her as she walked toward the door, pulling off her apron.

"Fine. Yuck. I hate it back here. It's so hot." Julie reluctantly slipped on an apron and picked up the spatula.

Blinding sun assaulted her eyes as she opened the back door. The community pool was busy this time of year. She had no idea there would be so many kids with nothing to do but go to the pool and swim every day. Not like her childhood, if you could even call it that. Wasn't like Justin's either, she thought with a pang of guilt.

Classic management move to keep the supplies for the kitchen in the office building, but it did allow her out of the hell hole every once in a while to breath some fresh air, albeit chlorinated, still better than what she was breathing near the grill.

Making quick work to gather what she needed, she did several trips back and forth, restocking everything that was low. On her last trip back, she did a quick check of the front and noticed the condiment stand was a mess. Taking a deep breath, she ran to get a wet rag and went back to clean up what Julie and Tami were supposed to keep clean. *Those girls were serious slackers.*

After cleaning the condiment stand, she checked the rest of the front set up to make sure there weren't any disasters looming. Satisfied there weren't, she headed back toward the kitchen.

"Shane!" Tami shouted from the cash register with an order ready to be picked up.

"I'll get it, Tami. What do they look like?"

"Tall, dark hair, slight beard, cut like you've never seen, red trunks—with three kids," Tami reported, searching the tables, "Over there." She pointed.

Rowan grabbed the tray piled high with food and several drinks, before walking over to a table full of kids.

"Is anyone hungry over here?" she asked.

The kids jumped up with shouts of, "me, me, that's mine, over here!" as she started passing out the food. Once all of the kids seemed to have what they had ordered, she had one corn dog left.

"And this must be—" turning her attention to the dad Rowan's words died in her throat and her heart almost stopped when his dark brown eyes collided with hers. For the first time, Tami was absolutely accurate in her assessment of a customer. He had short dark hair, almost spiky, with a smattering of a beard, and sitting there in his wet board shorts he looked cut like a god. His abs alone made her mind go places she hadn't been in years. His shorts were riding low enough to see a happy trail running along his flat stomach, straight down his perfect V and ducking underneath the waistband of his shorts.

Clearing her head, she realized she was holding her breath. He looked familiar, but then she wasn't thinking clearly at the moment. The exquisite male before her reached up and gently lifted the corn dog boat from her hand.

"Thanks. That would be mine." His voice was deep and rich and slithered across her skin, causing her arms to break out in goose bumps.

Rowan froze, feeling her throat instantly dry up as if she hadn't had water in days. She could rationalize her dry throat, that was to be expected in this heat, but the goose bumps suddenly appearing on her skin could only be explained by her sudden, intense reaction to this man. *Damn, I really need to get out more.* Embarrassed, she tried to pull herself together.

"If there is anything else you need, just let the girls know," she croaked out as she turned and all but ran back to her place by the grill.

Humiliation crept into her veins as she realized how childish she had just acted. Feeling the heat of it crawling up her neck and blossoming on her face, she blew out a breath, disgusted with her behavior. After all this time she expected more from herself; she was a grown woman, for heaven's sake, and should be able to have a conversation with a good-looking man without turning into an adolescent. Drooling over fathers spending a day with their kids was not acceptable. Might even be a new low for her. After all this time, working so hard to fit in and act like a normal woman, with a normal background and history, all it took was one fine man and she still felt like an awkward teenager with too many hormones.

Not that she was anywhere near giving up, but she was getting impatient with herself. She would never go back—that was a given. But, the outside was, in fact, a lot harder than she thought. She knew Jolly was evil and cruel, but maybe he did know a thing or two. Out here was confusing and hard, with too many rules and expectations.

Rowan took a long drink of ice water and a deep breath. She may be thirty-one with no outside skills at all, but she was fierce and determined to make it. She was already running the Snack Shack for the community pool—HA! Proof that she could handle it out here. Rowan smiled at the thought. Besides, she had Justin to think about. Failure was not an option.

• • •

Shane sat holding his corn dog in the air, stunned at what had just happened. He couldn't believe his luck. The girl! His girl—the one he'd been trying to meet for weeks, was working here of all places. When she handed him his lunch, he got so lost in her eyes, he didn't want to come back. They were the brightest hazel he'd ever seen, and they glowed as if a light was shining within, making them appear almost yellow. When their eyes locked, it was as if she looked straight into his soul. He shivered at the thought.

He noticed her the day she'd moved in and had been trying to talk to her ever since. He thought it would be relatively easy, given that they lived in the same apartment complex, but he'd been so wrong. She moved like a cat and he always missed her. He even considered stalking the mailboxes, figuring she had to get her mail at some point, right?

When Shane first saw her, she took his breath away—and that never happened. Dressed in old tattered jeans and a tight black tank top, he couldn't stop watching her. As she carried in her boxes, he kept expecting her friends to show up and help her move the big stuff. As far as he saw, no one ever came and she never really moved in anything big.

At first glance he thought she was young, like just out of high school young, the way her body rippled with muscles as she carried her boxes up the stairs and the spring in her step as she practically skipped down the stairs empty handed to get more. Her silky brown hair was cut short, just hitting her chin line in the front, tight in the back. She looked like an athlete or a fitness model. But after watching her for a while, he decided she wasn't that young after all. She had the kind of beauty that gave most women confidence, but she never looked anyone in the eye when they passed on the stairs and never once stopped to talk.

He had watched her move in all her stuff, never once venturing out and offering her help or hospitality. He'd been kicking himself ever since. What a dickhead move that was. He could have manned up, introduced himself and offered her help, but he just stood in his ground floor apartment all day, mesmerized by her, like some creepy stalker. Just when he'd realized his mistake and was about to venture out, his phone rang and his whole life got turned upside down.

"Uncle Shane!" his niece Jennifer screamed, pushing a French fry in his face.

"What's up, sweetheart?" he asked her, coming out of his daze.

"Eat, silly." She plopped a handful of fries into his paper boat.

"What's wrong?" his nephew Jake asked. "You look funny."

"It's that lady," Aaron added, before inhaling his burger.

Of all of his sister's kids, he related to Aaron the most. Shane vividly remembered being nine. Just at the cusp of being cool, but not quite old enough to pull it off. Jennifer, the oldest of the group, was a lot like their mother: organized, bossy yet caring. At eleven, she had already perfected the art of getting her brothers to do what they needed to do without making them feel like she owned them. Jake was seven and a handful on a good day. Why or how he agreed to watch them for two weeks while his sister and her husband enjoyed a second honeymoon was beyond him. At day three, Shane wondered if he was really going to last another eleven days, but hey, who's counting?

"Do you know that lady?" Jennifer asked him.

"No, sweetie. But I think she lives in our complex. I guess I just didn't expect to see her here. That's all. Go ahead and eat so we can get back in the pool."

He sat back and ate his disgusting corn dog in three bites. This is what he remembered doing as a kid. Hanging out at the pool, eating pool food, and soaking up the sun. He and Melanie spent more time in their community pool during the summer than anywhere else. That's where he learned to watch people. He learned to recognize the difference between fear and excitement when kids jumped off the diving board. He watched teenage boys square off silently when they were both eyeing the same girl. He watched in awe as his sister's friends evolved from play mates to real girls, and as his friends changed their own behavior around them. All skills he used on a regular basis as a Private Investigator. He loved being a PI. Knowing early on he was never going to be a desk job guy, and that he didn't follow orders very well, he'd never aimed for a traditional career. In high school he learned that he could blend in almost anywhere and had a face that people rarely remembered.

Between that and his theater classes in college, he soon became one of the top investigators in the area. The only down side was, at 32, nothing surprised him and trust was a rare commodity in his world. Other than casual relationships along the way, he'd never had what he would call a girlfriend, never met that one girl who took his breath away. Not until now, anyway. And he didn't even know her name. He needed a name to go with that face and that body. He needed it now.

He stood abruptly causing all three kids looked up at him nervously.

"Keep eating, guys, I'll be right back." He nodded his reassurance and turned toward the snack bar.

It was time for him to man up. He was a PI for God's sake; at the very least he could get a name.

"Can I help you?" The young girl at the window fluttered her eyelids and smiled at him. Shane chuckled as he remembered his own hellish teenage years.

"Yeah, hi." He turned on his most charming smile. "I was just wondering. There's a lady who works here, she just brought us our food." Shane waited.

"Oh yeah. That's our manager, Rowan. Is something wrong?"

"Nope. That's great. Rowan, huh? Thanks. That's all I needed." He turned, a genuine smile on his face.

"Hey, wait Mister," the girl called, and he turned back. "What's your name? Seems only fair, right?" She smiled coyly at him.

"Uh, Shane," he told her, impressed with her

forwardness, "My name is Shane Adams. Have a good one." He nodded to her and left to go back to his charges.

• • •

Climbing the steps to her apartment, Rowan thought of nothing else but peeling off her clothes and taking a nice, cool shower. The complex had a small pool, but she needed to get the smell of old meat and grease off her skin and out of her hair. Then, maybe if the pool was empty, she would sneak down and take a quiet dip. The last thing she wanted to do was get in a pool with a bunch of screaming kids.

Luckily, there seemed to be few children in this apartment complex. After doing as much research as possible, she had decided Oakdale would be her next step. She knew that Justin was set for a while longer, maybe later this summer he could come visit her, but the days when it was the two of them against the world were long gone. Truth be told, she liked it better this way. It seemed as if she had spent her whole life taking care of somebody, and just being in charge of herself was a nice change. Knowing that Justin was safe and far away from Jolly was enough for her. He was living his life, she was living hers.

She was thankful for her job at the pool, but knew that it was only for a couple of months at best. One of these days she would get a real job that didn't involve grease and slime, but until that happened, she would stick with fast food. It was better than the shady under the table work she had when she first started out.

Summer was short lived and the kids would be going back to school, the teenagers she managed would be back in high school, and she would be, once again, out of work. She needed to find something to do that was easy to pick up and move. Maybe bartending, or construction. She knew a lot about construction, she knew nothing about bartending, or drinking.

Walking into her apartment always made her smile. She knew, without a doubt, that this was her safe place. Having moved several times now, she knew exactly how to make her home perfect for her. Not too sparse, but not so cumbersome that she couldn't pack up and move quickly. Always keep moving! That was the key to her survival. At least for the first few years. She knew that going in, but it was worth it. Worth every inconvenience, every box lost or destroyed, every item left behind. Her freedom was worth all that and more. Jolly be damned — this was her life.

She peeled off her clothes, throwing them in a plastic bag. They smelled so bad, she didn't want them stinking up her apartment. This was her life and she loved it, stinky clothes and all, but there was a limit.

~

The cool water moving across her skin as she dove into the pool was heavenly. Having put her laundry in the washer, she planned on swimming till they were done. The laundry room was just across the way from the pool, so doing laundry was as easy as taking an evening swim. She'd always wanted to be a swimmer when she was a kid, now she got to indulge with each and every load of dirty clothes.

Coming up for air, she pulled herself out of the pool and sat on the side. It was still hot outside, but with the sun almost down, it was nice to just sit and enjoy the warm air drying her suit.

"Nice night." The deep voice penetrated her

thoughts and she darn near fell back into the pool.

"Oh! You scared me—" She turned and came face to face with the father of three from the pool. "Shane?"

His face lit up when she said his name. Tami had not let up all afternoon about the hot dad that wanted to know her name, and how awesome was Tami that she now knew his. It had gotten on her last nerve.

"Hi Rowan. So the window girl told you I came by, huh?" She could hear the amusement in his voice.

"Yes, she did. Your daughter's not old enough to be annoying yet, so I guess I shouldn't blame you for asking Tami, but for heaven's sake, she would not let up." Rowan slipped back under the water.

Why was he here and why was he talking to her? She was so flustered, she couldn't think straight. She had to breathe at some point, so when she got as far away from him as possible she came up for air.

"—not my daughter." She heard when her ears cleared.

"I'm sorry. What?" she asked, still flustered.

"I said Jennifer is not my daughter. Neither are the boys. I'm the crazy uncle that agreed to watch them for a couple of weeks while their parents rekindled their relationship in Hawaii." He looked right at her, waiting.

"Oh." Rowan let that soak in for a second. "Wow, you are crazy! I take it you don't have kids of your own?"

Shane simply shook his head.

Rowan laughed out loud, "So you had no idea what you were signing up for, then. Well, you're in for it now."

He grinned, stirring infernal heat deep inside her. The promise of that grin made her toes curl; she had never seen anything so sexy in her life. With no other recourse, she dove back under the water to pull herself together. Popping up back on his side of the pool, she pulled herself out of the water and slicked her hair back.

Taking a moment to look at him fully, she noted how comfortable, casual and edible he looked, standing there in worn jeans and a t-shirt while she was nearly naked, a fact not lost to her. His muscles called to her, and the way his fingers dangled elegantly from his hands made her mouth water. Oh, what were those fingers capable of? She tried to clear her mind before meeting his gaze, but from the look on his face, she guessed she wasn't as quick as she'd hoped.

He smiled as if waiting for her to have her fill. Chagrined, Rowan turned, grabbed her towel, and headed out the gate. "Good luck!" She called over her shoulder as the gate slammed shut.

CHAPTER TWO

Shane was reminded again that he was blessed with the best mother in the universe when she offered to take the kids for the weekend. He was so grateful, he vowed to send her the biggest bouquet of flowers every month for a year. All three happily packed up and left with her not two hours ago. He knew he had a lot of work to catch up on, but for now he was meeting up with Rob and Cody, his two business partners, at Bilbo's, the best place in town to kick back and have a beer.

Walking in, a cool blast of air and the smell of beer hit him in the face. The combination made his insides relax; muscles he didn't even know were tense went slack, and a genuine smile played across his face. He was ready for some much needed down time.

The pretense of meeting Cody and Rob tonight was to walk through some old cases looking for clues on some current ones, but they all knew that the real order of business would be cold beer and talk of women. At least, that's how it usually went down.

Bilbo's was busy tonight, with a long line of people waiting for tables. That was to be expected, being Friday night and all, but tonight there seemed to be a bit more chaos than usual. Shane walked in past them all, glad not to be in that long line. As soon as he got within earshot of the bar, he knew his friends had arrived—he could hear their boisterous laughter.

"Well well, if it isn't Adams himself." Rob noticed him first and handed him a tall glass of amber liquid.

"Hey, you've been keeping yourself scarce these days." Cody turned toward Shane, still leaning against the bar.

"Scared more like it. The kids are with me through the end of next week, get used to it." Shane drank a third of his beer. "Ah. Now that's more like it."

Cody and Rob laughed, drinking from tall glasses of their own.

"Where're the little rug rats now?" Rob asked.

"With my mother. Thank Fuck." Shane leaned into the bar, "Those guys are exhausting."

They laughed at him. He looked like hell and he knew it. It felt so good to just stand here and drink a beer—no fighting, no tickling, no worrying about why it was too damn quiet.

"So, what's up?" Shane asked, hoping they would stop laughing at his domestic situation.

"We were watching a beautiful creature across the bar when you walked up and disturbed us," Cody said, nodding his head toward a young woman. Shane almost spit out his beer when his eyes followed Cody's nod. It was Rowan. She was sitting at the bar with what looked like five mixed drinks in front of her. What the hell?

"Shit. That's my neighbor. She moved in a while ago, I just found out she works at the pool. What's she doing?"

"No way, man. I call dibs. I was here first." Cody

put down his beer and straightened up to his full height.

"Bullshit." Shane laughed back at him. "I've been chasing that chick for weeks."

"You're both pathetic, she's too high class to go for either of you fucks," Rob said, looking across the bar, watching her.

Shane turned his attention back to Rowan; she was sitting at the bar, taking tiny sips of each drink in front of her and writing down notes in her notebook. Just then, the bartender made eye contact.

"So, what's up with the lady across the bar?" Shane asked him as he wiped down the counter in front of them.

"The lady says she wants to learn how to tend bar. She's been here over an hour taking notes and drinking. She's drinking more now than taking notes."

"How many drinks she had?" Shane asked, concern in his voice.

"I think I've only cleared a couple away. You know her? She keeps going like this, she may need a ride." The bartender moved away to the next customer.

Without thinking, Shane got up and walked over to her. He didn't know her that well, but he knew where she lived and where she worked. He figured that was enough.

"Dude." He heard Rob, but he kept going.

"Hey, Rowan. What's up?" Shane casually idled up to the bar at her side.

Rowan turned her head around and smiled when she saw him. He could tell by her glassy eyes that she was pretty far gone — too far to drive for sure.

"Shane. What're you doing here? Where are those kids you're in charge of?" Rowan shook her head a little, as if to clear it.

"They're with my mother and I'm having a drink with some friends. We noticed your little experiment here." Shane watched her closely.

Rowan's eyebrows shot up in confusion only to relax as recognition set in. "Oh, this?" She indicated her drinks at the bar and laughed. "I need a new job. The pool gig is only going to last so long, and it stinks so bad back there! So I thought I'd check out bartending." She almost slurred her words.

"A new job, huh?" Shane glanced around, taking in the room. He noticed Rob and Cody watching him. He also noticed several other men watching them as well. So much for that second beer. He was getting her the hell out of there. He made eye contact with Rob and nodded toward the other men. Rob nodded back.

Turning back to Rowan, he said, "So, you think bartending might be in your future?"

"Oh man. I don't know. It's all so complicated. And there're so many drinks to remember. I've been watching these guys for a while now." Rowan looked so serious, he almost laughed. She had that sexy cute thing going on, the way she tossed her head back to get her short hair away from her eyes, a move she had done almost ten times just since he sat down.

"Yeah, I can see that. It's a lot easier if you're not sampling the drinks, though." He reached out and brought the nearest drink to his nose. *Whoa!* He didn't know what it was, but it was strong. "How many of these have you had?"

She looked at him again, her eyes a little clearer this time. There was something in the way she looked at him that made him freeze. Was that fear that just crossed her face? It was too dark in the bar to see her eyes that clearly.

"Shane. I'm not drunk. Don't even think about

trying to take advantage of me. Never going to happen." She sat up straighter and puffed out her shoulders. She also glanced around the room, taking in the men watching her, and Rob and Cody. "Friends of yours?" She asked, her eyes clearer still.

"Yeah, actually. I'm supposed to be having drinks with them. But I came over here to check on you. It's not every day a beautiful young woman sits at the bar with five drinks in front of her." Shane watched her take in the bar and noted how quickly she seemed to sober up. If he wasn't mistaken, she might have checked the exits too. Interesting.

"So sorry to keep you away from your friends. Looks like I need to get going now." She waved her hand at the bartender and pulled out her wallet. "I need to settle up. Thanks for your help."

The bartender smiled and took her money. "Anytime ma'am. Anytime."

Pushing her stool back to stand, she swayed a bit.

"Easy there. Doesn't look like you'll be driving anywhere tonight." Shane caught her and pulled her close, whispering in her ear. Holding her so close to his body was intoxicating; she felt luscious in his arms. He wondered if she felt his body heat up with her touch.

"Oh really? Are there taxis in this town?" Rowan tired to pull away, but Shane held her close to him.

"No," he whispered. "I'll drive you. Just let me say goodnight to my friends."

This time when she pulled back, he let her go. When their eyes met he watched hers go from open and curious to cautious. He could tell she was wondering what his angle was. She may look the part of the innocent, naïve young thing, but up this close, Shane recognized a sophisticated knowledge of life in those bright brown eyes. She looked so young on the outside, but her eyes told a different story.

"Well, you know where I live, so I guess you're as good a taxi as any." Rowan took a step back and waited for Shane to turn and leave. He paused, wanting to see if that fear crossed her eyes again. When he was satisfied that she was okay with this, he turned and lead her back to his friends.

"Rowan, I'd like you to meet some friends of mine. Cody and Rob, this is Rowan," Shane said as he approached them. He could tell they were trying to hide their shit eating grins. Assholes.

"Nice to meet you, gentlemen." Rowan reached out her hand and smiled. "It would appear as if I have had a little too much to drink this evening, and Shane has offered me a ride home. Thank you for allowing him to leave your get together."

Shane noticed she was back to her elegant self. With perfect manners, she shook their hands and greeted each of them. As he watched her, he saw her surreptitiously find the three exit doors and even note each window, making him wonder how such an elegant lady knew how to scan a room for exits and trouble.

Cody and Rob slapped him on the back as they left. With a mumbled promise to return later for food, he slipped out into the evening air and guided Rowan to his car.

• • •

Nice going, Ro. Rowan took deep breaths of the hot air, hoping it would clear her head. Steady, steady, steady, the mantra repeated itself over and over again as they walked to Shane's car. She was almost screaming it inside her head by the time they got there. She'd had entirely too much to drink. What the hell had she been thinking?

"You okay?" Shane asked again when he opened her door.

"Yeah. Thanks. I don't know what happened in there. Thanks for showing up when you did." Even after berating herself for showing such poor judgment, she felt safe with him. She didn't know why she did, but it was a nice feeling and she didn't want to question it. Sliding into the seat, she leaned her head back and started to relax again.

Shane went around and slid in the driver's side. She smiled when his scent reached her, making her skin tingle. She was just drunk enough to let her guard down and enjoy it.

"Not sure bartending is really in your future." She heard the amusement in Shane's voice and laughed out loud.

"Maybe not, but I gotta come up with something. Better than selling skincare products—believe me. Tried that once." Rowan laughed at the memory. "So, I was selling like mad. Then a customer wanted to practice on me, so I said sure. She used all her products on me and I broke out in a huge rash." Laughing too hard to continue, she snorted, trying to hold it together. "You should've seen the look on her face when she washed off the make up. I guess I looked really bad. She wanted to call 911. I spent three days on the couch underneath a coat of chamomile lotion."

Shane started laughing too. "Really? I guess that didn't go over so well, huh?"

Rowan looked at him. "Nope. Shocking what happens when the thing you're trying to sell turns you into the elephant man."

With the window rolled down and the warm air rushing against her skin, she almost felt giddy. "Can we keep driving?"

She put her arm out the window and tilted her head to get the full blast of air on her face. She heard Shane say something, but couldn't make out what it was. She was having too much fun. All of a sudden she was overwhelmed with the idea that this was freedom. This is what she had been searching for all this time. She laughed at herself and her ridiculously profound, enlightened state. Oh, the benefits of drinking! Opening her eyes, she noticed the car coming to a stop.

"Where are we?" she asked, looking around. Rowan knew she was nowhere near home.

"We're at the lookout," Shane said, and climbed out of his car.

Rowan swung her door open and climbed out too. He was in front of the car admiring the spectacular view of town. Although a while after sundown, the fading summer light collided with the mountains, creating a breathtaking image. All the more inviting with Shane centered in the middle of her view.

"Wow," slipped out underneath her breath. His jeans fit his ass perfectly, and his shirt fell just below his belt line, accentuating every single muscle. He was fit, that was for sure, she already knew that — seeing him at the pool in his board shorts had almost killed her — but now, with his tight t-shirt stretched across his strong shoulders, falling loose at his waist accentuating his perfect shape, Rowan was quivering at the thought of getting naked with him.

Whoa girl, snap out of it! Damn alcohol. Oh yeah, bartending is so out. She walked up next to him to see what he was watching so intently. Her eyes scanned the small town. Funny, all those people down there, scurrying away like ants. Living their lives, running from one place to another, looking for the meaning of life.

"You feeling better?" he asked, his eyes cutting sideways to her.

"Yes. Thank you." Not really, but she wasn't going to admit that now. Her entire body was alive and craving, begging even, for Shane to reach out and touch her. She waited, staring at the view, but not really seeing anything. Her senses were overwhelmed with him, her awareness of him, his scent, her need for him.

After a few minutes, Shane moved away from her and she held back a frustrated sigh as she listened to him walk back to the car.

"You coming?" he asked as he opened the door.

Tension swept into her veins. She shook her head, laughing at herself. "Yeah. I'm coming." Guess she read that wrong.

The ride back was not nearly as euphoric as the ride there. Her joy was tainted by embarrassment over how desperately she wanted to throw off her clothes right there at the look out—thank God she didn't. She'd have to move again. Laughing at the thought, she turned her attention back to Shane. Spiky hair, strong jaw and perfect lips, he looked like a bad boy, but sure didn't act like one. Leave it to her to find the one and only bad boy who behaves.

"What?" Shane asked her after a few moments.

"You, Mr. Shane, are a puzzle." She let out a breath she didn't know she was holding.

He looked at her, "Really? Me? I'm the puzzle. Talk about the pot calling the kettle black," he said, laughing.

Rolling that around in her head, she wondered

where she had misread him. She'd been pretty out of it when he first got to the bar. The alcohol was fading from her system now, leaving behind a dull throbbing in her head. She breathed out a sigh of relief when their apartment building came into view.

"So, listen. Thanks for being my knight in shining armor. I really owe you on that one. Please extend my apologies for the interruption to your friends," she said, sitting up, trying to compose herself.

Shane pulled in and parked. He had yet to say anything back to her, and Rowan wondered if he was angry. He simply got out and walked around to open the door for her. She was moving slowly enough to let him, and as she moved to get out Shane stopped her, coming to stand between her legs.

"Don't think for one minute that I didn't want to ravage your body at the lookout, Rowan." He moved in close and whispered in her ear, his body pressing in on hers. She shivered involuntarily. "When I do, cherish and ravage you that is, I want you stone cold sober."

As if warm wax dripped into her blood with each syllable, her body ignited at the sound of his voice. She leaned forward, pressing herself further into him, tilting her head to give him better access to her neck. Shane brushed his lips across her neck and along her jaw. Once again, she gave into the shivers running along her spine.

And then he pulled back and stepped away from the car. Completely stunned, she couldn't move. Finally, after what felt like an embarrassingly long time, she reached for his hand and made her way out of the car.

"Thanks for the ride. See ya' around," she managed to get out, sounding somewhat composed, before turning and heading up the stairs alone.

• • •

"What've we got?" Cody asked, crouching in behind the dumpster.

"We got a missing person in there," Rob answered him in a stage whisper.

"Then why the hell are we hiding behind the damn garbage can?" Cody asked. "Let's go get him and go back and finish our dinner."

Rob laughed at his friend. "See, that's what I don't get about you. You're a damn good PI, but you never like to get dirty. How does that rate?"

"Shut the fuck up, Rob." Cody opened his jacket and pulled out his gun. Getting ready for the next step.

"Hey, pussies. Shut the fuck up and get your head in the game." Shane knew this was what they did, but he needed it quiet to think.

Missing persons were always tricky. Some people were being held against their will, but most of them wanted to be missing, and would do anything to stay that way. As far as he knew, the guy in this hotel room was well loved and had a home and family waiting for him. But, his state of mind could be anything. No one really knew why he disappeared, so they had no idea what they were about to walk into.

"What do we know?" Cody asked Shane.

"My source says in and out of this room for a few days. Three unidentified women have come and gone, never more than once. That bike is his. That's what got us here. He got a speeding ticket this afternoon." Shane clipped off the details as if reading a grocery list. In truth, he was thankful that the call came in tonight, when he didn't have the kids to worry about.

"This afternoon? And the loser's still here?" Cody asked.

"Yep," Rob joined in. "That's why we think he's ready to come in. But just in case," he held up his gun, "Be ready."

"You bet," Cody answered and checked his gun.

Shane pulled out his Glock 9 and checked it, nodded to his friends and started moving. The group split up, Shane and Rob going toward the front and Cody taking the rear. Rob stayed at the stairway, as Shane continued to the room. He passed Cody at the back stairs and smiled. This wasn't the first time they finished a case in this motel.

Shane dropped his hand holding the gun to his leg, bracing his arm out of sight. He knocked twice. "Mike?" he shouted.

And waited.

Nothing.

He put his ear to the door and listened. "Mike, you ready?"

A groan came from inside the room. He leaned his head back and indicated to Rob and Cody to join him.

"Mike? Can you open the door?" Shane called again.

All three waited a beat, but when nothing came from inside, they knew they'd have to break the door down. Shane stepped out of the way and let Rob step up. He jiggled the handle, then stepped back. Without warning, Rob threw himself on the door. The door popped open and the three men burst into the room, guns drawn.

The smell of stale Jack Daniels and smoke hit him hard in the face along with a few other scents Shane preferred not to identify. Mike was passed out on the bed, alone. Cody cleared the bathroom and all three men tucked their guns in their holsters.

"Jesus," Cody said, looking around waving his hand in front of his nose.

"Oh man. Looks like the fun stopped awhile ago." Rob reached for the window and opened it.

Shane walked over to the bed. Mike was naked, clutching a bottle of Jack, vomit and urine covering his body. Shane nudged his shoulder and reached over to check for a pulse. As he leaned over to pull his wrist up, Mike swung widely, barely missing Shane's head with the bottle.

"Sonofabitch," Shane cursed, ducking.

Rob reacted lightening fast and jumped on the bed, pinning Mike's arm and yanking the bottle from his grasp.

"Fuck y'all. Leave me the fuck alone," Mike moaned from underneath Rob's large body.

"Dude," Shane spoke up. "Get up, the kid is covered with shit."

Rob jumped up and looked down. "God damn it!" He stormed off to the bathroom.

Cody stepped up and threw a glass of water in Mike's face.

"Shit!" Mike stuttered, sitting up.

"Yeah. So Mike. You need to get your shit together. How close are you to alcohol poisoning?" Shane asked, calmly.

Mike's eyes looked around the room. "Huh?"

"Shit. He's close. We should just call it in and let the medics take care of it," Cody said, watching him.

"Yeah, but hold on. I want to know why he ran." Shane got close enough to touch Mike's face. "Mike! Are you in trouble?"

Mike's eyes stayed closed. Shane looked over at

Cody who was pulling out his phone; he held up a finger asking for another minute. Turning back to Mike, he raised his hand and slapped him hard across the face.

Mike's eyes popped open again. He looked right at Shane. "What the fuck is happening, man?"

"Mike, are you running 'cause you're in trouble, or you just running?" Shane asked again.

"No man. I'm just living, man. I'm living my own life." Mike's eyes slowly started to close again.

"Call it in." Rob said from behind them. His pants had wet spots on them, but he looked clean.

"Yeah. He's just a stupid kid. Boy is he living though, 'cause this is the bomb," Shane said sarcastically.

Cody dialed and started talking to the 911 operator. Shane pulled out his phone and called his client. Mike's mother and sister would be relived to hear that he was alive and not in trouble.

Paramedics, motel managers, police, and a large crowd of curious onlookers all watched as Mike was loaded into the ambulance. It would take a good while for Mike to dry out. His sister and mother were on their way from Sacramento, overjoyed at Shane's work. The way they saw it, Shane saved him from himself in the nick of time.

Cody and Rob were giving their statements to the police. Shane had been interviewed first as lead investigator, so he was waiting for his partners. The local police all knew of him, but they still didn't like it when they ran into each other. The family hiring Shane was an insult to the authorities, but Shane finding him near death was a slap in their faces.

"You did it again, Adams." Sergeant Brookes walked up to Shane.

"What? Did my job?" Shane asked, wary of where this was going.

"Kicked our asses. We've been looking for this kid for a few weeks now. The only question I have to ask is, what took you so long? Timms said you got this case a couple of weeks ago." John Brookes leaned against the car that was holding him upright and smiled.

Shane looked at him for a minute and realized that he wasn't catching shit this time. "Been a little busy on the home front."

Both men waited, looking across the parking lot at the scene in front of them.

"Yeah, that sounds more your speed. Next time, just do me a favor and give me a heads up, will ya?"

Shane's head jerked up at his request and he drew in a breath to tell him to fuck off.

"Now hold on, Adams. I'm not going to get in your way, I just want to be in the loop so I can smooth out the ruffled feathers your good work causes in the department. I personally don't give a rat's ass who finds 'em. I just want 'em found. Just keep me in the loop so we don't step on each other." Brookes paused and pushed off the car. "Who knows, it might be the start of a beautiful relationship."

He laughed at his own joke as he walked away, not waiting for a response. Shane watched him disappear in the chaos, chewing on this new piece of data. Cody and Rob walked up.

"Let's bounce." Rob looked anxious. "I need to get the fuck out of these clothes."

"Maybe you should look before you leap next time." Cody razzed him.

The men laughed as they walked back toward Shane's car, happy to have closed another case.

CHAPTER THREE

"Uncle Shane!" Jennifer screamed, her voice reaching a high enough octave to break glass if sustained. "Where are you? Aaron's done peeing, we can go!"

Excellent. Shane was in for it now. He should've left with them two hours ago, and the kids were antsy and hungry.

Right one cue, "Shut up, Jennifer. Next time you go to the bathroom, I'm going to announce it to the world." Aaron's words cut into Shane's brain like a knife.

Looking down, he noticed Jake standing at his side. "Uncle Shane, I really want to go to the big pool now. Have you found your person yet?" The little boy's innocent question did him in.

No, he hadn't found his missing person and he wasn't going to sitting at his desk. He needed his sister to come back and take her children so he could think. But none of that was going to happen, so he pushed his chair back and stood.

"Let's go swimming before your sister and brother kill each other," Shane told him, causing Jake to squeal as he walked out of the room.

On the way to the pool, he called Cody and told him what he'd figured out so far, asked him to chase down some leads while Shane played nanny at the pool. He had less than a week left, but he was anxious to get back to work. That made him feel guilty about his lack of enthusiasm for his niece and nephews, so he turned up the volume on their favorite radio station.

With music blaring and all the kids singing at the top of their lungs, he pulled into the pool parking lot. His stomach flipped at the thought of Rowan. He checked his teeth in the mirror and ran his hand through his hair. Only to turn and see all three kids watching him closely.

"Are you getting ready for pool babes?" Jake asked with a grin.

"Pool babes?" Shane stuttered back to him.

"Yeah. Ya know, babes that hang out at the pool, prowling," Jake stated matter factly.

"Prowling," Shane repeated. His eye went to Aaron. "What have you been telling your brother?"

Aaron threw his hands up, "Don't look at me!"

After a moment of silence, they all starting laughing and Shane climbed out of the car. The kids followed him, grabbing towels, hats, and sunscreen.

It was only after they settled in and the kids were happily swimming in the pool that Shane started to relax. There were moments like this where he thought he might be able to hack this parenting thing. There were others though, when he thought he should be locked up and never let out for even thinking he could handle two weeks of parenting, let alone a lifetime. No wonder his sister needed a break. It was the least he could do.

With one eye on the food stand and one eye on the kids, his thoughts turned to Rowan. He hadn't seen her in a few days and didn't know what to think; he told her he wanted to kiss her, hell, he told her he wanted to ravage her body — only when she was sober. She had turned on a dime and walked away from him without a word. He meant it to be romantic and provocative. He didn't want her to think he would take advantage of her inebriated state, but after thinking about it, maybe she took it as an insult.

He groaned a little thinking that she might be staying away from him because she thought he didn't want her because she was too drunk. He checked on the kids one more time and then made his way to the food stand, his heart pounding and his hands sweaty. Jesus, he was a mess! What was it about this woman?

"Hiya, Shane." The girl in the front smiled at him.

Momentarily confused about why she knew his name before he recognized her as the girl he had asked about Rowan, he smiled back, hoping to get some more information from her.

"Hi there. Rowan in there hiding?" He leaned on the counter, purposefully flirting with her. One thing he knew was how to get information out of a young, pretty thing.

"She's not here," she cooed back at him.

"Really?" He was a little shocked. Why wasn't she at work? "Where is she?"

The counter girl laughed. "Running late, I guess. They never really tell me anything. All I know is she's not here yet, but will be soon. We're to just do our thing and if something comes up, just push it off till she gets here."

"Something bad, huh. Like running out of hot dogs?" Shane was stalling, hoping to get more out of her. He smiled again, laying it on thick.

"Yeah," she tossed her hair and smiled at him. "Like running out of hotdogs."

Shane went in for the kill. "So, wow. Do you guys run this place on your own a lot? Seems like a lot of responsibility for someone so young."

"Hey. I'm not that young ya know. I know a lot about a lot of things." She almost pouted. Oh, this one was going to be trouble when she grew up. Shane knew the type.

"I'm sure you do, sweetheart. So you run this place, then?"

She looked at him and her eyes narrowed a little. "No. Actually, this is the first time Rowan's ever been late. She's like, married to this place or something. But I know she'll be proud of what we've done without her. We even have Julie cooking back there."

Getting what he wanted from her, he backed away. "Well, I'll let you get back to it then." He turned and went back to his chair. He angled it so he could watch the front gate and the kids at the same time. His PI side was on high alert, and he wanted to know what was up with his Rowan.

• • •

Rowan paced the parking lot, checking her watch one more time. This wasn't like Talia or Justin, they should have called already. She was late for work and needed to leave. Why this place, of all the places she could have gone, why did they pick this place for her to wait? This was a No Tell Motel that rented rooms by the hour. Yuck! How Talia found this pay phone she would never know. If only she would call already.

There had to be a better way to communicate with each other. Everyone else had cell phones, but she was terrified Jolly knew how to track those. She knew postcards were the safest way — even if they were slow and unreliable. Maybe she read the date wrong or something? She headed back to the car to pull the letter that came in the mail yesterday. Yesterday. That was cutting it close, wasn't it? What if she hadn't received the letter in time?

Pulling the car door open, the heat pushed out, reminding her that she should be at the pool sweating in front of the grill, laughing at her teenagers' jokes about boys and music. She reached in and pulled out the letter.

"Hey, little lady. You waiting for someone?" The smoker's raspy voice startled her and she whipped her head up to see an overweight, aged biker. He had a long beard and wore a leather vest with patches sewn haphazardly on the sides.

Rowan rolled her eyes; this was the last thing she needed. She had to get back to the pay phone in case it rang. "Yeah," she told him soberly while trying to push past him, but he wouldn't move.

Trapped by the car door and the biker, Rowan ran through her options and waited.

"Where do you think you're going? I'm trying to have a conversation here." He leaned into her, his nasty breath overwhelming her nostrils.

Holding back a gag, she leaned in closer to him. "You are? And here I thought you were trying to pick me up. I am so sorry," she said in a high pitched voice, and even feigned a laugh. "So, what you wanna talk about?" She tossed her head just for good measure.

The biker relaxed and smiled. He moved back a bit, letting her escape her trapped position between him and the car. She closed the door and quickly locked it, then leaned on the hood, feeling the heat through her jean shorts.

"What's your name, sweet cheeks?" He puffed out his chest, giving her what he must think was a sexy stare.

"My name's Cassie. And I have to go back to that phone over there cause my boyfriend's about to call me there. Do you mind walking me? There're so many scary people around here." Rowan made sure to make each statement end with a question. She started walking back to the phone with the biker at her heels.

As they walked across the parking lot, she scanned the area. There were seven cars, three people in the office, and two men on the balcony watching them. She made eye contact with one of them. They looked familiar, but she couldn't place either one. Both of them looked too well dressed to need to keep company at a place like this. *Shows you what I know about the real world.*

Rowan got close to the phone and turned to thank her new 'friend'.

"Well, thanks so much. I'll just wait for the phone to ring. Should be any minute now."

"So, your boyfriend's calling you here, huh? Seems like a funny place to make your girlfriend wait for you. I'm thinking he doesn't like you very much." He sneered, leaning into her again.

She checked her watch then noted the time on the letter. She hadn't read it wrong; something must have come up. Neither Talia nor Justin were calling today. It was time to leave.

The biker reached out to touch her face and Rowan reacted without thinking. She grabbed his wrist and twisted it; bracing it on her shoulder, she brought him to his knees as he cried out, loudly.

"So listen, buddy. I'm going to let you go and you're going to walk away from me. And next time you better think twice about unwanted advances. Got that?" She tightened her hold and he fell a few more inches. "I'm sorry, I didn't hear you?"

"Yeah. Yeah. Son of a bitch," he bit out. She released him and looked up to find the two men from the balcony running toward her.

Oh great. Just what she needed, more attention.

"You okay?" the first one said as he approached her, "Cody, grab that son of a bitch."

She watched as the other man, Cody she assumed, threw himself on the biker as he tried to get up. They landed on the pavement with a loud thud.

"I'm fine. Thanks boys. Y'all can go rescue someone else." She turned to leave.

"Hey, don't I know you? I'm Rob, remember, from the —" He started to follow her.

Rowan didn't know where they knew each other from, but she knew they did and she needed to get the hell out of there — fast.

"No. No. I'm not from around here." She yelled over her shoulder and scrambled to get into her car. Revving the engine, she bolted even before rolling down the window.

As her tires peeled, throwing up rocks, she steered the car as fast as she could toward the pool. After a few blocks she slowed enough to roll the window down. Drawing the cooler air into her lungs refreshed her and started to calm her nerves. She knew she had to get her head on straight before going to work. One thing about those girls, they may be young but they were so darn perceptive. Rowan couldn't stub her toe without the gang sensing it and going all out to help her through it.

Pulling into the pool parking lot less than 20

minutes later, she checked herself in the mirror one more time. Running her hand through her hair and wiping the sweat from her forehead, she stepped out and shook her head to clear it.

As soon as she walked into the gate she ran into Julie.

"Where have you been? You okay? You look a little, I don't know. What happened?" Julie rushed toward her. Rowan knew it was just a matter of time now, Julie's loud teenage voice carried across the pool.

Katie stuck her head out the side door, "Oh, thank God you made it. I'm dying in here."

Rowan couldn't help but laugh. "Sorry guys. Just some family stuff. I'm here now. Thanks for helping out! Katie, I'll take over.

The next few hours flew by as Rowan tried to keep up with the orders and make up the other work she missed. Before she knew it, the pool was closing. Katie and Tami were cleaning up the tables while she started shutting down the back. Even with all the work she had piled up, her mind kept coming back to the missed phone call. What was up with Justin and Talia?

"All clean out here, Rowan." Tami called to her over the counter.

"Thanks guys. You girls go on home. I'll take care of the rest of this. I need to restock and do some paperwork." Rowan paused long enough to look up at her. Tami had a funny look in her eye. "What's going on out there?"

"Oh nothing." Tami's voice was anything but innocent. Must be some cute boys. Rowan had been so preoccupied she hadn't left the hut all day.

"Okay then. Thanks for your help today. Tell Katie

thanks for me. See you tomorrow. Bright and early, I promise." Shaking her head, Rowan went back to cleaning the grill.

After the grill was clean, she needed to restock. Rowan was glad no one was here now; being able to prop open the two doors and not be distracted should make for quick work. She propped the back door open and headed to the office. She could still hear voices in the restrooms. Some families took forever to change and leave. It sounded like they were talking to each other through the bathroom doors.

"Hurry up, Jake. We need to leave, the place is empty now." Rowan heard a girl's voice pleading. Chuckling, she rounded the corner and came face to face with none other than Shane.

"Oh. Hello." Still in hospitality mode, she smiled without thinking about who she was smiling at.

He grinned at her and gave her a once over with his eyes. Damn, he really was sexy, standing there in his board shorts and flip-flops. Even his feet were sexy. The smattering of hair across his chest, his hard muscles just underneath his skin, his lean body, all of it called to her like nothing else ever had.

She stopped short, the smile fading from her face as the reality of his effect on her hit her full force. She knew she was staring; she just couldn't pull her eyes away from him. Her skin started humming while hot liquid pooled in her insides. When her eyes found his, she saw the same desire reflected back.

"Uncle Shane, get Jake outta there. I want to go home," the girl standing next to him whined.

Shane dragged his eyes from Rowan to the girl. "Yeah okay, sweetie." He turned back to Rowan, "Sorry. We're almost done," and slipped into the restroom.

"Hi," Jennifer spoke to her.

"Um, hi," Rowan said, shaking her head, trying to pull her thoughts back together. "Did you have a good day?"

"Yeah, but we come to the pool all the time now. No offense, but I never want to swim again."

Rowan laughed out loud. "I know what you mean. Cake is great once in a while, but all the time is too much."

If she could just remember what she was doing over here, she could get back to it.

"Do you run the pool?"

"No. I run the Snack Shack." With that, she remembered. She was restocking. Back on track. "In fact, I need to get back to it, otherwise I'll never get out of here. Have a good night. I hope you get to go to a movie or something soon."

Rowan turned and went back to the office. She could still hear Shane and his family getting ready. The boys were not quiet by any stretch, and Jennifer seemed to be able to overwhelm them all with her high pitch, loud voice.

Walking straight to the back of the office, she leaned against the wall to catch her breath. She was not opposed to having a lover. In fact, she quite liked the idea. It had been a long while since she found anyone who could knock her socks off like that. After Colt, no one came close.

Colt. The last thing she wanted to think about in this moment was him. Sorrow started to replace the excitement in her lower gut. Shaking off the memories, she focused on the sexy man outside. For the first time in a long while she felt nervous, but a happy, excited nervous. Letting the feeling take over, she closed her eyes and remembered his body.

"Rowan, you back here?" Her eyes snapped open at Shane's voice. She stumbled toward the front before even thinking.

"Yeah, what's up?" She pulled in a deep breath to calm her nerves. Shane was standing in the doorway, a towel draped across his neck, but otherwise the same.

"Are you okay to be left here alone? The kids are ready and cranky. Otherwise—" His voice trailed off.

"No. I'm fine. The lifeguards are around here somewhere. Thanks. I'll see you at home though."

Shane's eyes widened in surprise. He tilted his head and looked at her. She could tell his brain was trying to sort something out, she just didn't know what, exactly.

"Yeah, okay," he said, turning to leave.

She watched him walk out and gather his charges. She felt a stirring deep inside and enjoyed the fantasy playing in her head of the two of them in bed. He seemed like the perfect guy to step out of reality with. She loved the idea of spinning a cocoon and stepping inside. She knew it would only be for a brief period, maybe until the end of summer, maybe a few weeks longer, if she was lucky. Heck, she'd take one night with him.

Depending on the word from Talia and Justin, she might even get a full month of bliss before packing up again and starting over.

CHAPTER FOUR

Two more days. Melanie and Graham get back in two days. Shane's clients were getting annoyed at his slow results thus far on a few cases, and he needed to get back to it. He had managed to pick up a few more missing persons cases, but while he played house he passed those on to Cody and Rob. He was done playing house. Never in his life did he ever think that taking care of three kids would be so consuming. He felt like his whole life was put on hold while he played at the pool, or went to the movies or the park. Kids. Never again.

Jake and Aaron were supposed to be playing a video game while Jennifer took a shower. They had plans for the water park today. Jennifer put her foot down and refused to go back to the pool. Somehow the water park was better? Kids. Never again.

Shane could tell from the noise level in the living room that the game had lost its appeal and the boys were starting to wrestle. That only meant one thing. A huge fight was about to erupt. He had maybe five minutes to track down his latest lead and get out there.

Just then, a loud wailing sound came from one of

the boys. He couldn't tell which one. But he knew his time was up. Kids. Never again.

"Uncle Shane. The boys are screaming again," Jennifer yelled from the other room.

He still didn't know why his neighbors hadn't complained enough to evict him. Maybe they took pity on him. He did make sure everyone knew that this was just for two weeks, then the rug rats would go home.

Shane walked down the short hallway to the living room to find the couch pillows strewn across the table and floor, a trail of blood heading off to the kitchen. Excellent.

Walking into the kitchen, he almost fell over. Rowan was standing over Aaron and Jake was getting a glass of water.

"What the hell?" Shane asked without thinking.

Jake turned toward him. "Aaron fell and hit his eye and blood came out. It was gross. Rowan came in and stopped it. Where were you?" The boy sounded wound up with all the excitement.

Rowan hadn't moved; her ass was barely covered in cut offs and her tank top climbed up her back. Shane had a full view of her tan, toned thighs and felt his dick twitch. His mouth suddenly going dry, he grabbed the water glass Jake just filled and drained it.

Handing it back to Jake, he walked a few steps closer to Rowan and Aaron. There were several bloody rags on the table and Aaron looked pale. Oh shit.

"Jesus, kid. What happened? And just for the record, the boys were supposed to be playing a video game and I was ten steps away," Shane added, defensively.

"Well, your day just changed course. You, my friend, are now going to go to the ER for stitches. His eye is cut pretty deep and that skin is really thin. Just two or three should do it," Rowan said, still holding an ice pack wrapped in paper towels to his eye.

Aaron started crying and Jake starting screaming for his sister. All the commotion was too much for Shane. His head ached and his heart started racing.

"Why the hell are you so calm?" he snapped at Rowan. "And how the hell did you even get in here?"

For the first time, Rowan looked up at him. She was so beautiful he stopped breathing. Even with all this chaos, he still couldn't help but picture her naked. How wrong was that?

"It's okay, Aaron. Your Uncle just doesn't know about these things. You're going to be fine. Besides, the scar will make you look like you just fought in World War One. You're going to look awesome."

"Oh, no fair!" Jake whined from the living room. "I want a scar too!"

"Don't even think about it." Shane turned to Jake as he was lining up on the couch. "One kid at the ER is enough."

"Jake, I need you to be my Ice Man." Rowan stood up. "Go get a bowl and put all the ice in it you can. We need to keep this as cold as possible while we get there. Jennifer, get dressed right now. We need to leave in two minutes. Aaron, hold this while I find the nearest ER."

Shane watched in awe as Rowan took over. Jake raced to the kitchen and started pulling ice out of the freezer. He could hear Jennifer in the other room racing around, getting dressed, he assumed. Aaron put on a brave face and held the ice pack on his eye.

"You coming?" Rowan asked him, suddenly in front of him.

"Ah. Yeah. I guess I better." His brain still wasn't fully engaged yet.

"Do you have their insurance cards and a letter authorizing you to treat?" Rowan asked him.

"What? Oh God. I don't know." Shane racked his brain. Did Melanie leave him with that? And then he remembered the envelope. "Oh wait. Yeah, I think so."

He raced down the hall to his office and pulled out the sealed envelope she had given him. Sure enough, there was the insurance card and a letter signed by both parents. He stuffed the papers in his pocket and grabbed his wallet. By the time he was back in the living room, Rowan had all the kids out the door and was headed to the parking lot.

"Shane, open your car," she called over her shoulder when he locked the front door.

By the time he got down to the car, they were all in and ready to go. He didn't even question how she did that; he just leapt in the car and followed her directions to the nearest ER.

Six hours and three stiches later, Shane gathered up the troops and left the hospital. So much for the water park; Aaron's eye couldn't be under water, and that meant movies and dry parks for the rest of their stay. To his shock and amazement, Rowan stayed with them the entire time. She seemed to know exactly what to say to Aaron to keep him brave and comforted. Jake and Jennifer roamed the hospital and had to be carted back a few times by the nurses, but for the most part they were well behaved.

All three kids were in the back, quiet and exhausted. Rowan was sitting up front, her tanned thighs calling his name. It took all his will power not to reach over and stroke her skin.

"So, um, thanks for being there. I don't think I could've done that without you." Shane glanced at her across the car.

"Well, it wasn't the day I had planned, but it was a day. The kids did great. Aaron is a brave little man. It was my pleasure." Rowan looked almost pensive as she gazed out the window.

"You seemed to know what you were doing." Shane wanted to ask her how she knew he needed three stiches, how she knew just what to say to Aaron, and how she knew how to wrangle all three kids. But something told him to wait.

Rowan laughed. "Not my first rodeo. You'd have been fine. I just happened to be walking by when I heard the howl. I knew that sound could only mean blood." She stopped abruptly and looked out the window again. "Anyway. I'm glad I could help out."

The mystery of this woman was killing him. There was so much he wanted to know about her. He watched her a second, then went back to watching the road.

"Hey, kids! I think we need to thank Rowan by making her dinner! Whatta ya think?" Shane glanced in the mirror to see the kids.

Jake and Jennifer popped up, "Yeah!! Let's get pizza and a movie!"

Aaron seemed pretty out of it and Shane didn't want Rowan to leave just yet; he wanted her around to keep an eye on Aaron. Flashing a grin at her, he realized he just wanted her around period. She was smiling shyly but when she saw him watching her, she laughed out loud.

"I guess pizza and movie it is," Rowan said. "I just want to change first. I was cleaning house, never really expected to be out today."

Shane laughed. "Is that how you clean house? You can come clean my house any time you want."

She playfully smacked his arm. When they pulled in

and parked, she helped Aaron into Shane's apartment and excused herself to go change. Promising to return, she disappeared out the door and Shane let out a breath he didn't know he was holding.

"You like her, huh Uncle Shane?" Jake teased when they were alone.

"You. You little — thing, you. You both should be in trouble for causing all this havoc. Go clean up the living room while I order the food. Jennifer, check on Aaron. I think that medicine they gave him is making him sleepy. And no more wrestling or rough housing! Your mother's going to kill me as it is." Shane walked into the kitchen to get the pizza shop's phone number.

Two days. That was all that was left. And now he was the uncle that left them alone and had to take Aaron to the ER. He groaned. Kids. Never ever again. He couldn't believe he had to call his sister and tell her about this.

After he placed the pizza order he walked into the living room to find all three kids sitting on the couch watching Finding Nemo. They looked like perfect little angels. Ha! He knew better. No wonder his brother in law was bald. He tore out all of his hair because of his kids.

"Pizza is on its way. I'm calling your mom and dad. Let Rowan in when she gets back. Get me if the pizza comes and I'm still on the phone." Shane talked above their heads, hoping their brains had registered his words. He knew that Aaron was out of it, but he hoped Jennifer and Jake were at least half listening.

With a deep breath, he picked up the phone and dialed the 808 number he had for emergencies.

"Aaron or Jake?" Graham's voice came on the line.

Much to Shane's surprise, he didn't sound angry or worried. "Aaron. Well, it was both of them, but Aaron has a few stiches on the corner of his eye, near the eyebrow. The nurses all told him he's going to look like Indiana Jones."

"Jake okay?" Graham asked, his voice still steady.

"Oh, yeah. He's fine. A little worried about getting in trouble when you get home. But only because Mel is going to have my ass when you guys get back. Look, Graham —"

"Shane. This is normal. These things happen. We know we asked a lot when you took this on. Melanie is fine. Well, she will be. I plan on telling her after drinks. Lucky for both of us, my office has forgotten the definition of emergency and this phone has been ringing constantly. She just assumed it was my office again."

Shane started laughing. Relief flooded his system. "Thanks, man. I'm really sorry. I was ten steps away. My place is not that big."

"Yeah, you'd be surprised what can happen in a blink of an eye. Well, we almost made it through unscathed. See you in a couple of days." Graham hung up before Shane could respond.

Shane laughed again. Graham didn't even sound surprised, like it was expected. He better get back in there, he didn't think he would get off that easy again. He was strapping these kids down for the next 48 hours. Nothing was going to happen, even if he had to wrap them all in bubble wrap. Was that considered child abuse? He didn't know, and he almost didn't care.

As he came out of his room, he heard Rowan's laughter floating down the hall. The sound washed over him, doing things to his insides. She blew him away today. Maybe all women just knew things, like how to take care of kids in the ER? Maybe Rowan was just that wonderful?

"Well well, looks like the pizza got here. I thought I told you to come get me?" Shane surveyed the room. Two pizza boxes were open, plates were strewn across the room, and there was already a mess on the floor. *How can they destroy a room so fast?*

"Oh. Sorry, Uncle Shane. Rowan showed up with the pizza and we dove in. It's really good." Jennifer wiped up whatever that was on the floor and moved back to the couch.

"Rowan got the pizza, huh? What happened to us buying her dinner as a thank you for saving our asses at the ER today?" Shane was now embarrassed, again.

Rowan got up and Shane's breath got caught in his throat. She was wearing black fleece pants that hung on her every curve and a loose brown top that fell off one of her shoulders. Her hair hit her chin line, accentuating her jaw and long neck. All Shane could think about was running his tongue along that same line. He knew he was in trouble.

She walked across the room and quietly whispered suggestively, "That's okay, Shane. You can thank me another way."

He was rooted to the spot. Did she just say that to him? Did that mean what he thought it meant? He turned his head and watched her ass disappear into the kitchen.

"Uncle Shane, come sit with us. I don't like the sharks," Jake called to him from the other room.

Shane wanted to follow Rowan into the kitchen and clarify what just happened. With a reluctant sigh, he walked into the living room and pushed his way between Jennifer and Jake. Aaron had moved to the overstuffed chair, half watching, half dozing. Poor kid.

Rowan walked back in and settled herself on the floor near Aaron. He reached out and touched her hair. Shane watched her lean into his touch and pat his hand. They seem to have really bonded throughout the day.

"Man. Nemo's dad should've just hired Uncle Shane to find Nemo. Then he wouldn't have gotten lost," Jake piped up, frustrated at the character's ineptitude.

"Really?" Rowan asked. "Is Uncle Shane good at finding lost fish?"

"No. Uncle Shane is a Private Eye. He finds missing people all the time. He carries a badge and a gun, even," Jake answered with reverence.

Shane was pleased that his nephew was so proud of his job.

"No, silly. Then Nemo's dad would've never met Dory and then we wouldn't get to watch their adventures," Jennifer schooled Jake.

"Yeah," Aaron joined in, "We would never get to meet the turtle dudes. I love the turtles."

"Wait." Rowan's voice was not at all amused or impressed. If anything, she sounded alarmed. "You're a PI? And you work missing persons cases?"

"Why yes, that is in fact what I do when I'm not babysitting these three hooligans." Shane tried to keep the humor in his voice, but he could tell something was up with her.

"Huh," she said, settling back down. "I never met a real life PI before."

With that, they all focused on the movie again. Shane glanced over at Rowan on more than one occasion, hoping to catch her eye. But she never looked away from the movie, never moved from her spot on the floor, and never even laughed at the movie with the kids.

Aaron was asleep when the credits starting rolling, so Shane picked him up and carried him to what was once his office. By the time he came back out to check on the other two, they were brushing their teeth. Rowan was nowhere to be found.

"Hey, did Rowan leave?" Shane asked them.

"Yeah, she said she needed to go. She said to tell you to make sure Aaron had medicine nearby, 'cause he might need some in the night," Jennifer answered after she finished.

"Oh, okay." his head was spinning. How did it go from her suggestive invite to her bolting while he was out of the room?

He wondered what he did wrong. Maybe he misread her tone? Maybe she was mad that he didn't follow her to the kitchen? Women? This was why he was still single at 32. But she was a mystery, that was for sure, and mysteries he could handle. Hell, he did that for a living.

CHAPTER FIVE

Rowan peeled back the postcard, her heart hammering in her chest. She knew the exact number of hours she had been waiting to hear from Justin. 51. That's how long she felt like she had been holding her breath. She hated that she was more and more nervous with each passing hour.

'Sorry we missed you. See you soon. JR' was scrawled across the back of the card in Justin's handwriting. Rowan blew out a breath. See you soon? And only signed by Justin. What about Talia? Staying put, I would imagine. She didn't enjoy moving around as much as Rowan did. Never did, really. They were truly cut from different cloth. Must be their different mothers.

Why was Justin coming here? Why now? Rowan thought a different plan was in play. Something must have happened. She wished she knew more—like when he was going to show up.

And to top it all off, Rowan now knew that Mister Heart Stopping Sexy was a freaking PI. Of all guys to take notice to her, of all the men out there, why was she always attracted to the most dangerous of them? Dangerous for her heart, dangerous for her soul, and now dangerous for her safety.

Men. What a waste. Rowan rubbed her hands in her hair, trying to break her train of thought. Wishing for a different life was never going to solve the problem at hand. Sometimes late at night she allowed herself to wish. She wished so hard at times tears formed and wouldn't stop. If only Colt had bigger balls. If only she had been born in Wisconsin, a normal girl with a normal, boring life.

"Ahhh!" Rowan jumped up. "Enough! This never helps. Move. Move. Get up. Do something. Focus. Find a new job and quit moping. Don't go negative." Rowan spoke the words to herself as if she was chastising a teenager.

She needed to go for a run. It was hot, but the heat would be good for her. She changed into running gear, grabbed her safety bag—you never know. Never let your guard down. Never quit watching the streets. That's what she knew. That's what pulled her through her panic attacks and her night terrors. Justin was safe. And even if he wasn't, there was nothing she could do about it right now.

She glanced around her apartment. It was a mess; proof that she was getting sloppy. No way she could move fast enough with this mess, she was going to need to up her game. Damn Shane Adams and those distracting kids. No more. She couldn't risk having an affair with him. He knew how to track people, he knew how to spot a liar. He knew too much about hiding things.

She might need to move just to get away from him. But right now she needed to go for a run. After filling her water bottle she locked the door and headed out and down the stairs, forcing herself not to look at

Shane's door. She didn't want to know if they were there or not. She didn't know when their parents were coming, but she knew it would be soon. She knew Shane would only be preoccupied for a few more days, and then he would come find her. She needed to be ready.

Stretching out her legs around the corner from the apartment building, her thoughts drifted back and forth between Shane and Colt. Why she felt the need to compare them, she didn't know. Frustrated at her lack of control over her mind, she headed off. Holding back for the first few minutes, she didn't want to start too hard and blow out her legs again. That took weeks to recover from last time.

Slipping into her mantra: Breathe. Run. Breathe. Run, she hit her stride about a half a mile in. Soon though, her thoughts went back to Colt. She could admit it now, if only just, he broke her heart. She bared her soul, shared her forbidden desires and her deepest fears and when the moment came, he failed her.

She never expected him to falter like that. His words still rang in her head. *I'm not like you. I need this too much. I can't go with you.*

Rowan's heart squeezed at the memory and she stumbled. Snapping back to the present, she looked around, taking inventory. No one following, no one approaching her. Back to the mantra. *Breathe. Run. Breathe. Run.*

Breathe and Run. That was what her life had become. Colt may have broken her heart, but she didn't let it break her. She saved Justin. She saved herself. Jolly would never get her now. *Breathe. Run.* That's what she did; she took the time to breathe, and she ran.

Justin's letter said she would see him soon. That

meant they would be leaving again. She noticed she was almost at three and a half miles. Her legs were nice and warm and sweat covered her body; the wind she created cooled her as it brushed across her wet skin. Her shirt was sticking to her back and her hair was soaked at her neck.

This was bliss. Her bliss. No one could take this from her. No matter what, she would always be able to find this state. She remembered when she couldn't run. Confined to such a small space, but still she managed to get here. Yoga saved her then, and running freed her now. She smiled at the memory of being able to outsmart Jolly with her yoga and meditations. Wasn't it Gandhi who said, 'You can control my body, but not my mind?'

Four and a half miles; one more to go. She was pushing now and went into a full sprint for the last half-mile. Breathing hard, her legs felt like jello. Her muscles were starting to scream and her lungs burned. All sensations she lived for. Reminders that she was alive. She was everything he didn't want her to be.

At the five-mile mark, she slowed down and turned toward the apartment. She jogged another five minutes and ended right back where she started. Without thinking, she glanced over at Shane's door. He was watching her from the window.

Rowan's heart nearly stopped. She could see him from the street. Wearing nothing but shorts, she felt his body call to her even from here. Stopping to stretch, she tried to gain back some control over her breathing—not from the run, of course, but from the man behind the glass.

Would spending one night with him be so bad? Two nights? She didn't have much time anyway, he wouldn't have time to get attached. What did the teenagers call it, A Hook Up? Isn't that why she escaped — to live? To not be afraid anymore? Why would she deny herself this? She knew how to run and hide. If she could run from Jolly, she could run from anyone.

She looked up to see if he was still there. She smiled at him and waved. It took a moment, but he waved back. She put her hand to her ear, motioning for him to contact her. What was the point of life if you couldn't live it? Rowan was going to do exactly that. Starting with hooking up with Shane Adams.

• • •

Well, if Ms. Rowan Baker wasn't the most confusing woman he had ever come to know. She saves his ass with the kids, flirts with him shamelessly, bolts, and now just told him to call her through the window. She had so many moods his head was spinning.

He had planned to wait until the kids left and then track her down. But here he was waiting for his sister and brother-in-law to show up, and who comes up but Rowan looking so damn sexy in her tight pants and half shirt. She'd obviously been exercising; he could see her sweaty hair from the window.

What he hadn't expected was for her to smile at him. And then, did she ask him to call her? Did she give him her phone number? Did her hips sway a little more than usual when she walked up those stairs? His head was wrapped around this woman something fierce.

Shaking his head and laughing, at himself or her, he wasn't sure, he stepped away and turned his attention back to the chaos in the apartment. The kids were supposed to be packing and cleaning up.

Ha! The place looked like a suitcase bomb exploded.

"Um. Hey guys? What's the plan here?" he called down the hall.

Jake came running in from the kitchen, "That's all Jennifer's stuff. She's packing."

"Is that what we're calling it these days?" Shane laughed as Jake bolted down the hall to his makeshift bedroom.

Just then, Jennifer emerged from the bathroom with her hands full. Shane watched with amusement as she delicately placed her bathroom stuff: make up, lotions, special hair conditioners, and other bottles of god knows what in her suitcase. He laughed out loud as he realized the entire living room was full of her clothes, books, magazines, and notebooks, strewn across every available surface, but here she was protecting her make up bag. *Girls!*

He walked down to check on the boys. A belly laugh erupted as he took in the room. Two suitcases were on the floor; Jake and Aaron were throwing in their stuff with not a care in the world. Not one piece of clothing was folded or neatly placed. Dirty clothes, clean clothes, books, and toys, all a jumbled mess.

"Uncle Shane. Can you help us get Aaron's suitcase closed?" Jake piped up after tossing something overhand into the mess.

"Uh. Sure. But it might fit better if you guys folded something?"

"Huh?" Both boys looked at him like he just spoke in Russian.

"Nothing." Shane laughed.

After strong-arming the suitcases, he directed the boys to put everything else in garbage bags. He knew his sister would repack that night at his mother's house. She could get it to fit, somehow.

Checking his watch, he figured they'd be here already. Walking back to check on Jennifer, he heard a squeal. "Mom!" Guess they arrived.

"Guys, your parents are here," he yelled back to the boys.

As if a herd of elephants had been unleashed in his house, Shane pressed himself against the wall as the boys flew down the hall screaming. By the time he made it to the living room, all three kids were hugging both parents. He took in the scene and a momentary flash of regret washed over him. He was going to miss those rug rats.

"Hey, Bro." Graham broke first from the group and shook Shane's hand.

"Good trip?" Shane asked him.

"Yeah. Great trip. Again, thanks for doing this. There really isn't anyone else we could've asked." Graham's eyes conveyed an earnestness that Shane was trying to understand.

"Yeah man. No worries. You have three great kids. We had a great time. Didn't we?" Shane turned toward the kids.

"Yeah!" they shouted in unison.

"And when we went to the ER, Rowan came, and she is Uncle Shane's girlfriend who works at the pool." Jake started talking at hundred miles an hour.

Melanie raised her eyebrows at Shane in question.

"Neighbor. Rowan is a neighbor. She happened to come by when it went down and she was a godsend. Knew her way around the ER. And yes, she works at the pool." Shane tried to stem Mel's excitement about a possible girlfriend. He really didn't need his sister riding his ass about it.

"Yeah. And we had to go to the pool everyday to see her until I refused to go anymore," Jennifer said, with a pout.

"Really?" Melanie started to walk toward Shane. "Everyday, huh?"

"No, Mel. You told me to keep them active. Don't even start with me. Seriously." Shane tried to brush her off. But he knew what she was like. Once she got a notion, he'd never hear the end of it.

"Okay kids. We need to hit the road to grandma's house and let Uncle Shane get on with his life," Graham bellowed over the room in general.

That sprang the kids into a new realm of chaos. Jennifer started racing around the living room gathering up clothes and books and tossing them into her suitcase and purse. The boys bolted to the back of the apartment with Melanie at their heels.

Graham caught Shane's eye and nodded toward the kitchen. He turned and walked in.

"So, how's Aaron?" Graham asked quietly.

"Fine. His eye still has stitches in it. But you can go to your doc at home and get them out. The paperwork is in his suitcase." Shane waited for more.

Graham swallowed and nodded, his eyes darting all over the room. Shane braced himself for whatever it was Graham was holding on to.

"So, listen. I know this might not be the best time to ask, but—" Graham paused and then looked directly at Shane. "This trip saved our marriage. You have no idea how close it was. Hell, I didn't know how close I was to losing everything." Graham breathed out a long breath.

Holy hell. Shane felt his body tense up as he absorbed what Graham just told him.

"So, I was wondering if this could happen again." Graham looked pained as he asked.

"What? You mean will I watch your kids again?" Shane asked him in shock.

Graham nodded and Shane laughed, relieved. That was the big question?

"Hell yeah!" Shane ran a hand over his hair, "You scared me, man. I didn't know what the hell you were going to ask, but I wasn't expecting that."

Graham smiled. "Yeah. That was it. We realized that we need to just be a couple sometimes. And after what happened with Aaron, I didn't think you'd ever sign up for this shit again."

Shane could see Graham's shoulders relax, relief pouring off him. "HA! That's funny. After that, I didn't think you guys would ever let me! Naw man, the kids are great. A lot of work, but fun. Maybe next time, closer to a week. My job really suffered. But I'd love to have them again."

"Thanks man. That is really going to help." Graham turned to leave.

"Hey Graham, my sister okay?"

Graham smiled, a genuine smile he hadn't seen in a few years. "Yeah man, she's great. We just needed to reconnect. It's all good."

Shane watched him walk out. Wow. He didn't know what went down with them, but it sounded as if they had taken this trip in the nick of time.

Shane loaded the last of the luggage in the car and watched as the family piled in. The kids were a swirl of constant noise and commotion. After hugs, fist pumps and promises to keep in touch, the rented van slowly made its way out of the parking lot.

CHAPTER SIX

Three days. It had been three days since she saw Shane through the window and gestured for him to find her. She was beginning to think she imagined the whole thing. Or maybe he was just not interested.

The days were long and hot, the back of the Snack Shack was hot and greasy, her apartment was starting to smell like old hamburgers, and her car definitely reeked of something nasty. Rowan needed summer to end and a new job.

The pool was closing soon and even though she knew she could stay and work weekends until the end of Labor Day, that wouldn't be enough. She'd start looking for waitressing jobs again. Try as she might, she just couldn't get away from serving people.

She still hadn't heard from Justin. His cryptic message didn't give her a time. Just that he was coming. Pacing back and forth, Rowan felt like she was going to explode. It was too hot to go for a run, so she changed into her suit and grabbed a towel. She'd work it out in the pool.

The cool water glided across her skin, calming her mind with each lap. As she swam, her mind drifted back to Lina, her best friend. What was she doing now?

Was she happy? Pushing that thought out of head before it could fully develop, she kicked the water harder. Lina needed to be in the same place as Colt. Although she knew why Lina stayed, she still missed her. Lina never had the same curse as Rowan. Lina wasn't a Baker.

Swearing, she pushed her head above water, forgetting to breathe, paralyzed by her thoughts. One day, she would be able to remember all the good times with Lina. One day, she knew, she would be able to catalog each and every precious moment of her life before.

That was her goal, to be able to go back through her memory and pick and choose which memories to keep and which ones to lock away. Not yet. She wasn't able to go back there mentally without her body reacting, running.

Floating on her back, she got her breath under control, before resuming her workout. Back to her mantra. Breathe. *Run. Breathe. Run.* She flipped over and thought of nothing but her arms moving and her legs kicking, breathing every third stroke and doing flip turns at each end of the tiny pool.

Having no idea how long she had been in the pool, but feeling her legs and arms were jello, she paused long enough to notice surroundings. She could hear people on the pool deck talking and kids playing in the water. Still alone on the lap swim side, she had noticed a few people on the other side.

Pulling herself out of the water and walking over to her towel, she nearly jumped out of her skin to see Shane sitting by it. She stopped short, shaking the water out of her hair, trying to calm her heart rate.

"That looked like a nice long workout." Shane stood, handing her the towel.

Reaching out, she took it. After drying off a bit, she asked him, "Were you watching me the whole time?"

"I don't know. You were in the zone when I first came in. But I've been here a while," Shane answered her, his gaze steady on her eyes.

"Were you waiting for me?" Rowan asked, impressed that he would.

Shane smiled. "Maybe."

Rowan smiled back. "Maybe, huh. I thought I told you to contact me, not stalk me." Now she was flirting. Damn, it felt good.

"The kids left. Had to catch up on work. Now I'm here, and I don't remember you giving me a phone number." Shane's eyes skimmed down her wet body before darting back up to meet hers quickly.

"You wanna come up?" Rowan asked him, her eyes making it clear what she was asking him.

A grin spread over Shane's mouth slowly. "Yeah. That'd be nice."

Rowan waited a beat, soaking in that grin. She dried her hair a little more and smiled back at him.

Turning and walking out of the pool gate, she hoped the air freshener candle she lit before coming down to swim had worked. When she opened her door, she observed her small apartment from a visitor's eye, noticing the open space with little furniture. In place of a table, a cushion and small stool stood. In place of a couch, a couple of bean bags lay on the floor.

Without a television to anchor the living room, the space looked overly large, with only a small stack of paperbacks sitting in the corner. Small cardboard boxes partially filled with books and paper sat next to them.

Rowan heard Shane laugh behind her. She spun around, wondering if this had been a fatal error.

"Jesus, girl. This is how you live?" Shane's words flew out of his mouth, while he spun around, taking in the room.

"And that's bad?" Rowan asked him.

"No! Not at all. Just. I just. Wow, this is kinda cool." Shane seemed at a loss for words.

Rowan watched him take in her apartment and laughed. "I don't like to collect stuff."

"Yeah. I can see that." He looked at her and tilted his head as if he wanted to say more, but chose to hold his tongue.

She turned around, "I'm going to go change. There's some wine in the fridge. I do buy food and wine. Just not junk."

Walking down the short hall to the bedroom, she questioned her sanity. Her small bedroll on the floor screamed someone on the run. She went to the box with her clothes in it and grabbed a pair of underwear and a pair of shorts. Changing as quickly as possible, she went back to the living room, hoping to distract him before he took it upon himself to explore the rest of the apartment.

Rowan walked into the kitchen to find Shane opening a bottle of wine.

"Looks like you found the wine."

"I love what you've done with the place," Shane said after pouring her a glass.

"Yeah. I worked hard to make the place work with my eccentric personality." Rowan led him back to the living room and snuggled into a bean bag.

She watched as Shane lowered himself into his own. When he leaned forward to sip his wine, clearly uncomfortable, she burst out laughing.

"Come on, you have to maneuver your hips and lower yourself down enough to support your head. It's an art, really," Rowan told him when she had recovered enough to speak.

Shane glared at her, "An art?"

"Yeah. Here, let me hold your wine." She reached out and took his wine, placing both glasses on the floor. "Let me help you."

Rowan placed both hands on his hips, pushing him down enough to create back support. "Now, lean your head back. See, there's nothing better." She ran a hand through his hair as he leaned back and watched her.

"You ready for your wine?" she asked him, still standing.

He reached out and ran his hand up and down her leg, his touch sending a firestorm across her cooled skin. She waited, absorbing the sensations.

"You're quite the mystery woman, Rowan," Shane spoke, his voice low, rough.

"Oh, that's where you're wrong. I'm the most boring woman in the world. I have a plaque somewhere." She tilted her head back, pushing her hips closer to him as he continued to run his hand up and down her legs.

"Really. You don't have a couch, but you have a plaque?" His hand stroked her inner thigh.

"Well, you know. A couch you can get anywhere. An award—that you have to keep. It's a rule." Her voice was getting thick. With every stroke of his hand, her belly tightened, her blood thickened, and her clit throbbed.

Her knees buckled and she slowly straddled him, her hands caressing his hair and neck, while his hand traveled up her shirt, sliding across her ribs and stomach.

"I know you're full of shit. There's no way anyone would give you an award for being boring. You're so far from boring. Sexy, maybe. You might have an award for being sexy—that I could see." Shane's hand stroked up and down her back, reaching up and grabbing the back of her neck.

He sat up while pushing her down. His mouth met her neck as she lifted her head, giving him the access he desperately needed.

"No one ever gave me an award for being sexy. I swear that's true," she said, her voice so low and sultry, she barely recognized it as her own.

"That's a damn shame." Shane spoke into her neck, his voice vibrating across her skin, making her hormones incendiary.

She moaned as his hands slowly made their way back down to her shorts, his fingers working the button and zipper. Rowan's body came alive and was ready for more.

A loud pounding on the door startled both of them. Rowan's head snapped, her eyes wide with fear.

"Ro!" The voice at the door shouted.

Rowan froze as Shane watched her closely.

"Rowan. Open the door. It's Justin."

With that she jumped up and ran to the door.

• • •

Shane watched as Rowan leapt from his lap and ran to the door. Not what he expected her to do after that look of pure terror in her eyes when they first heard the pounding on the door.

He stood and adjusted himself. Not two seconds ago he was rock hard, but that quickly faded. He didn't know what the hell was going on, but he knew something was off. The back of his neck bristled and his hair was sticking up. Not good signs, he knew. He couldn't let go of that look on Rowan's face when they were first interrupted, pure, unadulterated fear.

"Justin!" Rowan said when she opened the door. "You're here!" She sounded pleased. Very pleased. Who the hell was this?

She moved back to let him in, and Shane's jaw dropped. In walked a tall, young man with bright green eyes and dirty blond hair so short it looked almost fuzzy around his head. He was built. Better built than Shane had ever been. He couldn't gauge his age, but damn if he didn't look to be in his twenties. Maybe older, if you looked at the lines around his eyes. Those were worry lines for sure.

"Justin, I'd like you to meet a neighbor of mine, Shane." Rowan made the introductions as she smoothed out hair and checked her shorts. So, he was just a neighbor now? Was he not seconds away from stripping those shorts right off her?

Shane reached out his hand, stepping forward. Justin eyed him with suspicion and then, at the last possible second before getting really awkward, reached out and took his hand.

"I'm Justin. Nice to meet you." Shane watched as Justin eyed the place, scanning down the hall. He recognized the move, looking for exits.

He raised his eyebrow at him and pumped his hand once. "Likewise."

They dropped hands and both turned to Rowan. Shane caught the look on Rowan's face. It was clear that these two were more than casual acquaintances. The look on her face was one of love and admiration.

Shit. Time to man up.

"I was just leaving. Nice to meet you, Justin. Rowan. Have a nice evening." Shane turned and headed to the door.

"Thanks for coming over, Shane," Rowan said as he closed the door. He waited a beat, but there was no noise.

Slowly, he walked back to his own apartment. The night's events had left him utterly speechless, or thoughtless, as the case may be. *What the fuck was that?*

Rowan was, in fact, a mystery. Quite a mystery — all her repudiation just made him more intrigued. And who the hell had just walked in her door? Someone she knew, that was clear. Someone she knew very well.

And who lives that way? Who lives with a stool for a table and bean bags for a couch. He wondered what was in the bedroom; did she sleep on the floor? And who was that guy? What was he to her?

His phone interrupted his thoughts, swearing as he checked the caller ID.

"Yo," he answered.

"It's going down wrong. We're at the corner of Broadway and Willow. Shit's going to hit the fan." Rob's voice was loud and clear.

"Yep. Be there in less than ten." Shane snapped his phone shut and grabbed his gun.

Dashing to his car, he raced to the corner of Creekbed and Willow, hoping that was far enough away. He checked his gun, this time taking an extra clip, and took off toward his friends.

This is what they did. They worked their own cases, but they were all a phone call away. They had each other's back. Shane slowed and crouched, listening to the street, scanning the area. He knew his buddies' MO, knew they'd be under a bush or a dumpster waiting for him.

Sure enough, he found them crouched under an open dumpster that looked like it had been forgotten by the trash company for a month. Shane snuck up to them.

"What's the plan?' he spoke in a whisper to announce his arrival.

"About fucking time, Adams." Rob shot him a smile.

"We got a misper in that house. Looks like she doesn't want to be here. Looks like she's being held by that asshole watching the TV," Cody told him.

Shane reached for his phone, sending a quick text to Brookes.

"What the fuck?" Rob asked him.

"Keeping the locals happy. A new tactic. Plan?"

"Plan is—Fuck. Nothing good. We go in heavy. But they're ready. I think this is something bigger. There're just too many men guarding the house for there to be one girl in there. There's got to be more." Cody strained his neck looking for more angles.

"Call it in?" Shane asked.

"Naw. They'd take too long. And besides. I'm getting paid to get that one in there. I'm getting that one. I just don't know what kind of hornet's nest we're going to kick up."

"Okay." Shane pulled out his phone again. Rob threw him another questioning look. "Just anonymous tip. Let's go in back, heavy but quiet. If we're lucky, we're in and out, no one even knows."

"Yeah, that's what I was thinking, too. But, we're going to need something to distract them," Cody said.

"Rob, you still got your fire cracker stash in your car?" Shane asked.

Rob smiled, "Always, man. I got that." He disappeared.

"Let's move. You and me, in and out. We move on the first pop," Cody said to Shane.

"You bet man. I've got your back."

Shane followed Cody, moving quickly. They backed

up behind the house and Cody handed him a mask. Shane pulled it on and waited for Rob to start blowing shit up.

With the first small explosion, movement in the house was immediate. Cody and Shane slipped in and moved, one after the other, to the bedroom. Shane could hear shouts and more fire crackers going off. They didn't have a lot of time. Cody struggled to get the door unlocked. Shane wanted to just break it down, but knew it would make too much noise.

The door opened and Cody slipped in. Shane waited by the door. *Come on, come on.*

"Shit. Shane, get your ass in here."

He moved in, not liking the idea of leaving the door alone. When he walked in, there were five girls chained to the wall. *Fuck.*

The girls were terrified. He lifted his mask and held his finger to his mouth. Pulling out his small bolt cutters, he started cutting chains. He heard Cody doing the same, but there was no way they were going to make it before the house got wind that the mess outside was just a distraction.

He glanced around the room and noticed the window was locked, but there was another door. He checked it. It was to a bathroom. He checked the bathroom window, small but open. Moving back to the girls, he took the first two who were free and led them to the open window. He shoved them out, one at a time. He could hear them huddling, waiting for him.

Just as he was ready to go out after them, Cody and the other three showed up. Cody locked the door and Shane pushed his way out the window. Damn, he barely made it out. His hips and shoulders were scraped, but he didn't feel it just yet. That would come later.

The explosions stopped outside and he could hear the men coming back to the house. One girl dropped out, two more to go. Another fell awkwardly, making too much noise. *Shit.*

One more to go and then Cody. He could hear shouts from inside the house and banging on the door. Cody shoved the last girl out and Shane caught her. At first he thought she was unconscious, but then noticed her eyes were open. His blood ran cold when he saw the vacant look in her eyes. Cody pushed himself through with a grunt. Shane held on to her as Cody gathered the rest of girls and started running back toward the cars. Shane could hear sirens in the distance.

The group rounded the corner when the first gunshot cracked just over their heads. All the girls dropped and screamed. Not good.

"Up up up. Let's go." Cody pushed them up. "Shane, car?"

"Creekbed and Willow," Shane answered as he dragged two girls with him.

Cody changed direction and headed off toward the car. Just then, Shane heard a man to his right, he turned to fight and Rob slapped his hand down.

"Easy," Rob said, grabbing the girl with the vacant eyes from him, picking up the group's pace.

"How'd it go?" Shane asked him.

Rob smiled; the guy was a pyromaniac. "Great until you guys started moving around like a group of elephants."

Another crack of gunfire blew past them. *Shit, where were the damn locals?* Cody rounded the next corner and Shane dragged out his keys. He beeped the lock and Cody threw open the door; all the girls dove into the car. Cody and Rob stood outside.

"Meet you at my place. We'll play hide and seek for awhile," Cody said.

Shane didn't wait. He knew his buddies could handle themselves. He shoved the car in drive and took off.

"Stay down," he told the girls. Some of them were crying, some looked hurt, and he knew that escaping took a lot of effort.

"Who's hurt?" he asked when he turned out of the neighborhood, slowing down a bit.

"I think my ankle is broken," one of them said.

"My shoulder is broken, but that was from before," another one spoke up.

Christ.

"Anything else?"

"Angie's not good. But we don't really know why."

Shane knew who exactly who they were talking about, "Okay. Hang in there. We're going to an office. We're PIs and one of you has a family that hired my buddy Cody to find you. I have no idea who. Hang in there, we'll get to a hospital soon."

He slowed down to stop at a red light and saw three police cars screaming toward him. *Looks like the gunfight attracted some attention finally.* His phone beeped.

Shane could guess who it was. He checked it and chuckled. It was Brookes. They had Cody and Rob and the men from the house. But no one knew where the girls were. As soon as he got the word things were safe, he'd contact him.

Pulling up to Cody's office, his phone rang.

"Yo," Shane answered.

"10-20?"

"Your office."

"You have an Angela Wright with you?"

72

Shane looked in the back seat; the girls were off the floor, but still all on top of each other.

"Is her last name Wright?" he asked dreading the answer. Angie sat on the seat, looking pretty beat up, her eyes still vacant, her mouth slightly askew. The girls shrugged. "I have an Angie. Not speaking right now. No one knows why. They don't know her last name."

"Saint George," Cody said.

"Roger." Shane pulled back on the road and headed off to the hospital.

With the girls delivered to the hospital, Cody and Rob got busy sorting out who was who with the locals. Shane was allowed a few moments of quiet to wrap his head around his night.

A cup of hospital coffee appeared in front of his face and he looked up to see Sergeant Brookes attached to it. Shane sat back and took the coffee.

"Thanks," he said and meant it.

"What a night. You guys did good work tonight." Brookes sat down next to him.

"Not me. That was all Cody. I was just back up." Shane took a drink. Hot, but almost tasteless. Perfect.

"Anyway, thanks for the heads up. When we got there, all hell broke loose. When we found the chains, we knew what had happened. Your two guys were playing cat and mouse with the bastards. I'm assuming so you could get the hell out of dodge with the goods." Brookes spoke without looking at him.

"Something like that. Glad it worked out." Shane put his head down and let the exhaustion wash over him. "I think I'm going to take off." He stood and downed the rest of his coffee. "Thanks for this. See you around."

Shane pulled out his phone to send Cody a text

telling him he was cutting out. One thing the night had accomplished was distracting him from the man who showed up in Rowan's apartment.

"Hey, Shane. Wait up." Rob jogged over to him. "Take me to my car, will ya?"

He nodded and the two men walked to Shane's Kia.

"We saw your girl the other day," Rob started once they got in.

"What girl?" Shane asked.

"The girl from the bar. Ya know, the one you took home a while back."

"Really? Where?" Shane's curiosity was piqued.

"Yeah, at first I couldn't place her, but then Cody was pretty sure it was her. She's a feisty little thing."

"What the fuck does that mean, Rob?" Anger spiked into his blood at Rob's words.

"Easy." Rob tried to calm him. "We were over at the No Tell, checking on a dickwad, when we noticed a biker dude following this cute chick. Next thing we know, biker dude moves in for the kill and your girl takes him down. She had it all taken care of before we even got to her."

"What? The No Tell? What the hell was she doing there?" Shane asked, shocked.

"We never got that part of the story. The biker dude said she was waiting for her boyfriend to call at the pay phone and he was just being friendly. She darn near broke his hand. He reached out and she took him out. Some special justitsu shit. It was awesome." Rob was enjoying the story as he told it.

Shane whipped his head from the road, "Are you telling me that Rowan took down an Angel? A big one? With what, jusjitsu?"

"Yup. That's what I'm saying."

"And she was waiting for a call at the pay phone?

From her boyfriend?" Shane asked, his mind racing with this new data.

"Well, that's what she told the Angel. But, she bolted as soon as we got there, so she could've just been blowing smoke up his ass."

"What the hell was she doing there?" Shane asked, almost to himself, as pulled up to Rob's car.

"I don't know, man. Thanks for the ride," Rob said, jumping out.

Shane pondered all the possibilities as he drove down the quiet streets. Pulling into his apartment and shutting off his car, he sat and listened to the silence.

Quietly opening the car, he slid out, glancing up at Rowan's. He stopped short, surprised to see that her lights were still on. He couldn't help but think this was the boyfriend that made her wait at a No Tell. Boyfriend? That just didn't sit right, but whoever she had in there was awake. He watched as shadows paced across the closed mini blinds. Rowan and this Justin were awake and pacing at three in the morning. And Shane wanted to know why.

CHAPTER SEVEN

Justin was falling asleep on the bean bag, but Rowan was wide awake and pacing. The news wasn't all that bad, but shocking. And strange. She just couldn't figure out what they were playing at.

"So I contacted Jewel, not Lina?" Rowan barked into the brightly lit room.

"No. Not Lina. Ro—it's 3:30 in the morning. I gotta go to sleep." Justin moved groggily from his bean bag and started to pick up stuff to take to the back.

"Yeah, okay. Sorry, I just don't understand why they're saying those things. Just tell me one more time." Rowan waited for him to start over with his news.

Justin sighed and turned to face her, his usually bright green eyes tired and faded. "You contacted Jewel because you're not making it out here, and I ran away from you to live with Talia. You want a meeting with Jolly to make amends, and want to come back and claim your rightful place," Justin spoke in monotones, then turned toward the bathroom.

"And that's it? There was nothing more?" Rowan asked again. There was something Justin wasn't telling her.

"No Ro, there's more. But I'm going to bed. We'll talk more after I've slept ten hours," Justin said, slamming the door.

With nothing else to do, Rowan pulled out his sleeping bag and set it up next to hers in the bedroom. Justin was right; she needed to go to sleep. She had to go to work in the morning. She just couldn't understand why they started such a rumor, and what their end game was. If Jewel was involved, it wasn't good. She really needed to protect Justin and Talia, something was brewing and she was going to need to find out what.

Justin walked out and collapsed into his bag. She watched him sink into his make shift bed and close his eyes. Only then did she feel bad about keeping him up this long. Sometimes she forgot he really was only a kid. After turning out all the lights and crawling into her own sleeping roll, she kissed his forehead.

"Thanks for coming, Justin. Sorry I kept you up so long," she whispered.

"Go to sleep Ro. Jeeze." Justin said, smiling as he fell asleep.

~

Rowan sat outside on the pool deck sipping exceptionally strong coffee. The air was hot and dry, even at this early hour. She had a long day ahead of her, but first she needed to get her head around Justin's news. She always knew they would come after her one day, but she thought this was an odd technique. Guilt really wasn't going to work, especially from the outside. Taking a deep breath, she looked around her apartment complex. They would never think to look here, but just in case, she was really going to have to move. Maybe even change her name. She'd have to start looking for cash only work again. One of the reasons she moved so often was that her paychecks and bank data could be tracked, but now even that was too risky. She had hoped that she could stay just ahead of them for a few years and then they would move on, give up.

Two things were clear: First, she was never going back. Ever. She would not, 'claim her rightful place'. Nope, not going to happen. Second, she needed to protect Justin and Talia. They were innocents in this, and Talia had kids to worry about. Justin was going to have to leave again. She needed a separate plan for him, a safe place where they would never think to look.

The best thing was his name. Justin Ross was a common name out here, so he could be lost in a sea of Justin Rosses. Hiding in plain sight. Rowan was a little less common, but Baker was a godsend. Talia, on the other hand, was a little harder to hide. But then Talia never had to hide; she never had the same lineage. Same father, yes, but it was their mothers that made the difference. Talia's mother never would've agreed to what Jolly had wanted. Different paths, different places, that one small factor made a life possible for her.

"Hey," Justin's voice interrupted her thoughts, making her jump. "Maybe you've had enough of that for now," Justin said kindly, sitting next to her with his own cup of coffee.

"Hey," Rowan smiled at him. Here in the light, his bright green eyes shone as if he had a light behind them. So similar to hers, only a different hue, so much brighter, so much clearer.

"You thought it through yet? Come up with a plan?

Have a counter attack ready, steps one through six written down someplace?" Justin teased her, looking around as if searching for the list.

"Funny, har har." They started laughing together. That felt good. Rowan's bones started to relax.

"Ro, it's going to be fine. My take? Jolly's bored and needed to talk about something. What better subject than those who have left him? Of course they're going to say you aren't making it. He doesn't want anyone else getting ideas. And they knew Lina wouldn't lie for you, but Jewel, she'll do anything." Justin laid his coffee cup down and sat back in his chair.

Rowan snorted, "I know. Believe me, you don't need to remind me about Jewel."

Justin leaned his head back against the chair and looked up to the sky. "So listen. Keep cool," he paused, "The guy last night. What was his name? Sean? Shane?"

Rowan stared straight ahead, knowing exactly what he was doing. They used to do that all the time to talk privately. While looking up, no one could read his lips. "Yeah, what about him," she grunted out.

"Well, he's watching us right now. Just thought you should know." Justin didn't move. Just looked up at the sky.

Rowan nodded.

"Okay. So don't be pissed, but what I didn't tell you last night is that Colt and Jewel are together now. Jewel has got him wrapped around her finger. So whatever you told him, they all might know now." Justin spoke quickly, but kept his casual appearance, leaning back against the chair.

Rowan stopped breathing. The blood rushed behind her ears so loud she couldn't hear him anymore. As if he'd betrayed her all over again, a hot knife pierced her heart, tearing it apart.

"Wait what?" Rowan asked him again. She was packed and ready to go. For a year, they had been making plans. Stashing food, money, and supplies in airport lockers every time they went to town. They had bus tickets, enough money to get far away, and it was time to go. Justin was waiting for them.

"Rowan. I just. I can't," Colt almost whispered.

She looked at him as if he had morphed into a cat. He might as well have. "Yes, you can. This is what we have been working toward for over a year now. I have to go. Justin is waiting for me. If I stay, I lose everything. You, the Instructory, Justin. Everything. You know I can't do that." Rowan was desperately hiding the panic in her voice.

"There's nothing out there for me. I've been there. You think it's such a great place, but it's not. There's a reason I came here." Colt blinked back the tears and brushed his long, blonde hair out of his face.

Rowan watched him. His shoulder length hair shaped his boyish face and square jaw. His lips that had made her feel things she never thought possible, those lips that were now telling her he was abandoning her.

"Colt. Why? Why wouldn't you just tell me you couldn't come? I have no choice here; it's not about what I think is so great. I have to go. I can't stay. I need to protect Justin. I need to get to Talia. I can't do what he wants. Not again. You of all people know that." Rowan's voice was climbing, getting louder, and the panic started to take hold.

"I thought I could, baby. I thought you could carry us both through. I'm not like you. I need this too much. I can't go with you. I just can't." Colt broke down in tears.

"I can't carry you through. I'm already carrying Justin. He's almost 16. If we don't leave now, I'll lose him forever. 16, Colt. You have no idea what they do to the kids here.

Jewel runs the whole show. She makes Saturday exercise look like a pizza party. I can't let her have him." Rowan felt her resolve creep back into her bones. *"I'm leaving. Are you coming or not?"*

She waited, her backpack on her shoulders, for her lover, her confidant, her friend, to decide if he was going to stay by her side as he promised night after night, or if he too was going to abandon her – like everyone else had.

Colt didn't even speak. He just looked down, tears running down his face, and shook his head slightly. Without a word, she turned and walked out into the night.

"Ro! Breathe!" Justin was screaming at her as he pushed her head between her legs.

She felt the blood drain into her head and she sucked in oxygen. Big deep breaths, in and out. The world straightened on its axis and she sat back up. Only this time, it wasn't Justin she came face to face with, it was Shane.

"Are you okay?" Shane was watching her, feeling her pulse.

Rowan's eyes widened in surprise and the world tilted again. She closed her eyes and focused on her breathing. She could hear their voices.

"What happened?" Shane asked.

"I don't know, man. We were just waking up, and then she just almost fainted?" Justin answered him as if he had no idea what was going on. He even ended his sentence with a question, like many of the kids did at school.

"Jesus. What the hell?" Shane swore.

Rowan felt her blood pressure return to normal, but didn't open her eyes. She needed to convince Shane she was fine, just a little lightheaded. And, she was still reeling from Justin's little bomb.

"Shane. It's okay. I was just up late and felt a little

dizzy. That's all." Rowan opened her eyes and looked at him. He was standing over her like a guard. He even had his body between hers and Justin's. Justin had been pushed back, but was still standing, at the ready.

"Jesus, Rowan. Did you eat yesterday?" Shane asked, checking her eyes.

Pushing his hands away, she sat up. "Yes, I ate. I just felt a little dizzy. It's all good," She said, reaching for her coffee.

Shane took a step back and turned to Justin who was standing up to his fullest height, glaring at him. The two of them faced off for a brief moment, eye to eye, before Shane nodded and turned to leave.

• • •

"Shane, wait," Rowan called after him.

He paused, *dizzy spell my ass.* Justin had told her something. He had watched as the boyfriend leaned back to tell her they were being watched. And then he told her something. He couldn't make out what the boy—that was more like it—had said, but it had an immediate impact. Shane had watched as Rowan froze and all the color drained from her face. It was as if she just forgot to breathe. Before he even got out the door, Justin was up in her face, screaming at her to breathe and shoving her face between her legs. He had to hand it to him, he seemed to know how to handle it—almost as if he had expected it.

"Shane. Thanks for coming over and checking on me. Justin is a relative of mine, he's used to my occasional fainting spells, but you moved pretty darn quick. Thanks." She smiled at him.

Relative? He couldn't hide the shock and relief he felt hearing those words. Throwing a glance back at

Justin, it hit him. Now that she pointed it out, he was embarrassed that he had missed it. Their eyes were the same shape and seemed to be naturally highlighted, making them pop, and they both looked at him intensely with that same glow. They also had similar posture, the same wariness in their shoulders. He watched as Justin scanned the area, just like Rowan had, looking for exits, people watching, or god knows what.

Why not just say this is my brother? None of this was making sense, but he was pleased to know that they weren't long lost lovers.

"Oh yeah, look at that. I do see a strong family resemblance. Your eyes are very similar," Shane said, smiling, feeling his shoulders relax.

As if Justin just got what the tension was about, he jumped back, "So um, yeah. I'm going upstairs now." He turned on a dime and walked away.

Shane could hear Rowan chortle. He turned to her and smiled.

"You're right, I was a little worried." He sat down next to her, glad her color was finally returning.

Sitting up, she peered into his face. "Hey, are you okay? You look really tired."

"Yeah. I was helping the guys with a case after you, um, kicked me out. It ran late." He sat back and admired her legs.

"Oh." She sat back too, but frowned. "Was it another missing persons case?"

"Yeah, in fact, it was. We rescued five women who were being held against their will for god knows what." He sensed she wasn't happy about that, so he went on the defensive.

Why he felt the need to justify his job was beyond him. She worked at a snack shack, for fuck's sake.

"Oh yeah?" She perked up. "Good for you. Did you get the bad guys?"

He laughed. "Yep, the police got the bad guys. We just took the girls."

"So, you were out late with a bunch of girls, huh?" she said, blatantly flirting with him.

"Yes ma'am. After you kicked me out, I had to do something with all that pent up energy." He smiled back at her, using all of his will power not to reach across his chair and stroke her inner thigh, the memory of his hands on her taking center stage in his brain.

"Oh! Is that how it is, then?" She stood up, but the head toss she threw his way made her intentions clear. "In that case, I better go."

He stood up just as she walked past him. Their bodies were so close he could smell her shampoo and feel the heat waves coming off her body. His skin prickled, as if it was reaching out to touch her.

"I'll see you soon, right?" He leaned over and looked directly in her eyes.

"Yeah." She held his stare. "I'll see you soon."

For a moment they stood like that, just centimeters from each other. He could smell the coffee on her breath and see her rapid pulse rate in her neck. Wanting nothing more than to kiss her, Shane stopped himself. He was afraid that if he started, he would never stop. Taking a breath, he stepped back to let her pass. He watched her turn and start up the stairs. She never turned back; she just walked up and opened her door. But he did admire her ass the entire time.

• • •

"Are you insane?" Justin's words assaulted her as she walked in the door.

"Excuse me?" Rowan jolted out of her reverie.

"That man is a PI! I heard the whole conversation. Saving women my ass. That man could work for Jolly. He could be looking for us!"

"He doesn't work for Jolly. He's a really nice guy who just spent the last two weeks with his sister's kids. He's fine and he doesn't know anyone. And besides, when the hell do I discuss my love life with you?" Rowan spat back at him.

"Well maybe if you had, Colt wouldn't be a problem right now!" Justin shouted back at her.

"That's cold, Justin Ross. And you are crossing a line you don't want to cross." Rowan glared at him.

She went into the kitchen to wash her cup and get ready for work. After a few minutes, when she thought Justin was calm enough to talk, she tried again, "So what's the plan? Are you staying here for a while? Did you hear back from any of the colleges?"

He drew out a long breath before answering. "I need to stay with you for a while. Talia's great, but I needed some space. And college isn't an option right now. Maybe later. I'll find a job."

Taking in his words, she waited. No college, no Talia's, no safety. This was bad. She needed to come up with a plan.

"Okay. I'm going to be looking for work too. This gig at the pool is only going to last a little while longer. Do you have a lifeguard certificate? You might want to get one this winter. The lifeguards work long hours here. Just a thought for next year." She paused to look at him.

Justin's hair was so short and spiky it looked almost fuzzy, and his sharp green eyes looked back at her while his wide, straight jaw and protruding Adam's apple screamed out manhood. This boy had grown up over the last two years, no question about it; he was definitely a man now. He was actually handsome, and she was proud.

"What?" he asked her.

"You're a man now. Wow. You look good, Justin," she said in awe.

"Thanks, Ro. You can stop embarrassing me now." He smiled shyly at her and walked down the hall. "I'll look for work while you're gone. I'll come up with something by the time you get back. Okay?"

"Yeah, okay. I gotta run!" She said as she ran out the door.

CHAPTER EIGHT

Standing in the tiny kitchen, Shane swallowed his last sip of coffee, thinking about what the next two days were going to be like. He had a lot of slow, boring work to do and wasn't looking forward to it. He knew he needed to start tailing Mr. Clark—strangest hire ever. What daughter hires a PI to find out if her father is having an affair? The wife yes, the daughter, not really—ever. But as a personal favor to Cody, he said yes.

And now he was looking at two days in the car watching some old dude get it on with his secretary. Cody was going to owe him big, that's for sure.

The knock on his door surprised him, but what shocked him more was opening the door to Justin.

"Hi," Justin said, looking confident and a little defiant.

"Justin," Shane said, slowly.

Justin stood outside the door, tall and built. Shane just couldn't pinpoint his age. He looked like a teenager, but his eyes had the look of someone who knew the dark secrets of the world.

Justin laughed a little, "So yeah, can I come in?"

Shane waited a bit and then stepped aside, letting

SYDNEY HOLMES

him in. He walked in and looked around the apartment. It was the same basic layout as Rowan's, only this one was bigger, with a second bedroom and bathroom. It also had a couch and a real bed, but who was thinking about those details?

"So listen, I heard you work as a PI? And, I'm going to be around for a bit and need to find a job. Wondered if you needed any help?" Justin turned and looked Shane directly in the eye as he spoke.

Shane couldn't help it, he burst out laughing. This was not what he was expecting. He figured he was there to bust his balls about Rowan.

"Oh! Okay," Shane said, reigning in his laughter.

Justin's face tightened and his shoulders rose a bit. "I know how to handle a gun and I've done work like this before. Just thought I'd ask."

That got Shane's attention, "You do, huh? Sorry, I wasn't laughing at your request, I just expected the 'stay away from my sister' speech."

Justin looked at him, still tense. "She's not my sister. And yes, I can handle a gun, been training for a while. We all have been. I'm good, just don't have LPI yet."

That got Shane's attention. If this guy knew he needed one, he knew more than Shane thought. "Okay. What have you done?"

"Mostly trained. Did some tags and BEs. Never any mispers, though." Justin puffed up a little as he spoke.

"What the hell are those, man? I'm assuming you're talking about missing persons when you say mispers, very English of you, but tags and BEs?" Now Shane was even more curious. Where had this guy trained?

"Tags. Ya know, trailing people to see what they're up to. We called them tagging. And BE is breaking and entering — going into a space and searching it. A home, office, things like that."

"Whoa! Just to be clear, LPIs don't break into people's spaces, that's against the law. And Jesus, I don't know where you worked before, but that shit don't fly here. How old are you, anyway?" Shane looked stern as if reprimanding a child.

"I'm 18. But I know what I'm doing. Just try me," Justin said matter of factly, almost as if he had had this conversation a number of times before.

Shane stood back and assessed him. 18? How does a person get eyes like that in 18 short years? Might not be such a bad idea, hanging with the cousin, or whatever he was. He might get some more info on Rowan. God knows she wasn't flowing with information, and she was his greatest mystery these days.

"I have to tail Mr. Clark for infidelities. How are you at sitting still for hours on end?" Shane asked, thinking maybe he'd balk at that.

Shane watched as Justin took in his words. A smile spread across his face and his shoulders relaxed back down. "I'm good with that as long as you don't start singing show tunes."

Shane burst out laughing again. "Show tunes, huh. Who the hell have you been working with?"

"You don't want to know, believe me." Justin said, almost sounding like a kid again.

~

Several hours later, Justin and Shane sat in the dark blue Kia with tinted glass. Justin had sat the entire time, never once complaining, never needing a break or even a quick pee. Shane was impressed. Even Rob couldn't handle this long in the car without cracking annoying jokes or needing to get out and run or do push ups behind the vehicle.

Mr. Clark was in fact having an affair, but not with his secretary. The woman was a tall, dark haired beauty queen. They had pictures of the entire tryst. That was the one moment Shane was worried that Justin would get squeamish. But he just picked up the camera and took photo after photo; close ups of faces, pulling the camera back for atmosphere shots.

Shane had to admit, he was impressed. At 18, this kid knew what he was doing and did it professionally.

"These are good, kid. You take photography in high school?" Shane asked, trying to break the ice a little. Even after all this time, Justin didn't talk much — another trait just like Rowan.

"As a matter a fact, I did. Two years up north. Graduated as the editor of the school newspaper. I even won an award with one of my photos," Justin said while staring at the office building Mr. Clark had disappeared into about three hours ago.

Shane stopped looking at the photos on the camera. That was the most personal information Justin had divulged the entire day. Shane wanted to keep digging.

"Oh yeah? You graduate last June?" he asked, pretending to still look at the camera.

"Yep."

"So, what have you been up since then? Tagging and BEs?" Shane asked.

Justin laughed, "Naw. Just drifting. Trying to stay out of my aunt's way. Helping her with her kids."

Shane was processing that nugget of gold when Justin sat up.

"On the move." Damn if the kid didn't know his shit.

Shane started the car and Justin took the camera,

switching back from view mode, ready for whatever happened next. Shane watched as the woman who hired him and the beauty queen walked right up to Mr. Clark.

"Um," Justin said, before snapping photos of the three of them.

"Yeah, I see it." Shane knew then why she had hired him and not Mrs. Clark. Tiffany Clark was friends with the beauty queen and sensed something was up. He wondered if she had staged this little rendezvous for their benefit. So they could get photos of the two of them pretending to barely know each other.

Justin took pictures of the lovers awkwardly shaking hands, of Tiffany hugging her father, and of the three of them conversing on the street. After about five minutes, the two women left and Mr. Clark continued to the garage across the street.

Seven minutes ticked by before Mr. Clark's car drove out the exit. Shane slipped into traffic behind him and tailed him home.

"A little early to be going home," Justin commented.

Shane opened the file and handed it to Justin. As Justin read the report, he smiled. According to the information from his daughter, this was his normal routine. He never wavered from it. In the office by 8, home at 5. Which meant leaving the office just after 4:30.

"Nice. This guy has a cushy job. Barely works 8 hours and has nooners with a beauty queen from time to time. What a waste." Justin spoke with a disgust Shane hadn't heard before.

He noted it and saved it for later. He had to admit that after his time with Justin, he was now more confused yet intrigued with the pair of them than before. They parked two blocks up from a nice big mansion on a tree-lined street and watched Mr. Clark's garage door lower and shut.

"Well, that about sums it up. I think the client has enough, don't you think?" Shane spoke. He was getting anxious and wanted to get out and take a run. He knew Rowan's snack shack was closing at 5, and she might be home in about an hour. Maybe sooner.

"Yep. You're the boss," Justin said, sitting back in his seat, rolling his shoulders a bit.

Shane put the Kia in gear and drove out of the neighborhood. As they approached the apartment complex, Justin spoke again.

"So listen, it would be best if we kept this between us. I'm not sure Ro would, um. It would just be easier if you let me tell her. Okay?"

Another piece of the puzzle, interesting. "Yeah, sure. I'll let you handle Ro. You want to go out again?" Shane smiled.

"Yeah, whenever is fine. I'd rather be doing this than flipping burgers, so yeah, let me know." Justin smiled back at him. And nodded his head a few times, pleased with the progress of the day.

"You got a phone?" Shane asked.

"No. No phone. But I'll let you know where I am if I'm not at Ro's." Justin laughed dryly, as if the thought of having a phone was ridiculous.

They pulled into the lot and parked.

"Thanks, man," Justin said as he opened the door and jumped out of the car.

"No worries."

He watched as Justin bounded up the stairs and opened the door to Rowan's apartment. If he was curious about her before his day with Justin, he was even more so now. Justin had only managed to whet his appetite and he wanted to know more. Much more.

• • •

Walking into her apartment, Rowan smiled when the clean smell of Comet and bleach hit her. Ah, welcome smells after a day behind the greasy grill. Walking into the kitchen, Rowan found Justin mopping the tiny floor.

"Hey you. I see you haven't forgotten how to be a good 'Enviorator'!" Rowan laughed, using finger quotes to remind him of their old terms from back home.

"Oh god. Don't even go there. I'm simply cleaning because this place smelled like old grease and sweat—a lot like you, in fact," he said while rummaged around under the sink. "Here," handing her a plastic garbage bag, "Put those stinky clothes in this and hit the shower. You need a new job!"

Rowan laughed and took the bag. She wasn't going to disagree with him on any front. She stunk, the apartment stunk, and she needed a new job. She'd have to get on that, and soon. She saw the pool schedule today. The pool pretty much shut down after Labor Day.

As she let the warm water rinse off the grease and grime of her day, she let her mind wander back to Shane. She knew he was a PI, but she also knew he was a decent man and wouldn't hurt her. She still didn't know why, but she just knew that. She didn't trust him though; she'd never make that mistake again. But, she wouldn't mind a night underneath him. Her body quivered at the thought of it.

Things were just a little more challenging with Justin around. They'd have to leave the apartment, which meant that he was going to have to invite her over. As the water slipped down her body, caressing her inner thighs, her resolve got stronger. She would just have to invite herself over to his place. And soon.

She thought of Shane's dark eyes and short cropped, almost spiky, hair, his lean muscles and flat stomach, and of his masculine hands. She thought of Shane at the pool in his board shorts, a happy trail leading down his lower abdomen to underneath his shorts. She shuddered at what lay covered by the thin cloth. Yes, she was definitely going to invite herself over. Tonight.

She washed her short hair and stepped out into the heat. The evenings seemed to be the hottest part of the day here. The heat dragged on and on long after the sun went down. As if it was leaking out of the concrete that surrounded them, the heat penetrated long into the night.

Choosing shorts and a tank top, she dressed quickly, hoping to spend a little time with Justin before bolting to Shane's.

"You hungry?" She heard Justin ask from the kitchen.

"Yeah, but it's so hot. I almost don't want to eat anything," She called back.

"Ro. Come here," Justin shouted.

She sprinted into the kitchen. "What's wrong?"

"Nothing. Jeeze. I made a tomato and cucumber salad. I was thinking of going out later. Ya know, check out the scene. But thought we could eat first." Justin was stirring the bowl, looking perfectly relaxed.

"Nice." Rowan tried to calm her nerves. "Hey, how'd it go finding work today?"

"Ya know how it is," Justin said vaguely.

"Yeah. I know. I'm going to have to start waiting tables again. I tried bartending, but that didn't go well," she told him, as she gathered the plates and forks.

"You'd make a pretty good bartender. What happened?" he asked.

"I tried going to the bar and tasting the different drinks. Making notes. But ended up with a little too much tasting. Anyway, got my ass out of there, and that was that," Rowan answered him, a little sheepishly.

Justin stopped and looked at her, amusement clearly written all over his face. "You got drunk?"

Rowan could tell he was holding back his big belly laugh. "Oh, shut up!"

Justin roared with laughter. Rowan started laughing too. Thank God Shane had been there.

"You can thank Shane for driving me home. It was stupid, and just 'cause I did it doesn't mean you can," she scolded him.

"Shane was there?" Justin asked abruptly.

"He wasn't with me. He was there and noticed that I needed a ride." She trailed off, not wanting to discuss Shane with Justin.

"I hold my liquor better than you, anyway," Justin said as he served the salads.

"Since when do you drink, Mister?" She looked at him with what felt like her sternest look.

"Ro. I went to public high school. I've been drinking," he told her matter of factly.

Oh, she hadn't thought of that. He did have to fit in, after all. That made sense. She took her salad and moved to the bean bags.

"As long as it doesn't get out of control—" She started, but Justin cut her off.

"Don't," he said, a warning in his voice.

They ate in silence, each lost in their own thoughts.

The salad was good and just what Rowan needed. She forgot how caring and empathic he was with her. He always seemed to know what she needed. She smiled at him.

"Don't go there, either," Justin told her, smiling.

"I was just going to say thanks for the salad. It really hit the spot." She ruffled his fuzzy hair as she walked back to the kitchen.

The knock on the door made them both jump. Justin stood and waited. Rowan opened the door a crack and sighed when she saw it was only Shane.

"Hi." She opened the door all the way to let him in.

He stepped in and nodded to Justin, then turned his attention to Rowan.

"So, I was thinking, do you want to come back to my place for a while?"

Rowan's heart rate spiked, but she played it cool. Or thought she did.

"Yeah, well, you guys do whatever you want. I'm outta here." Justin put down his salad bowl and walked back to the bedroom.

"Justin. You don't have to leave," Rowan called down the hall. She looked at Shane and put up a finger, asking him to wait a second. She headed down the hall. "Justin. I'll leave. You stay here. It's okay. This is your place too."

Justin was shoving his wallet into his pants. "Don't worry about it. I need to bounce. I won't wait up for you," he said as he walked down the hall, grinning. "Shane." He nodded to Shane as he left and walked out the door.

Shane and Rowan stood looking at each other. In that moment, Rowan knew. Tonight would be her night with him. It was early, and for that she was thankful, because she wanted this one night to last as long as possible. Shane's eyes flashed at her as he seemed to read her mind.

"I guess we should go, then," Rowan said, a little more breathy than she intended.

Shane smiled and his dark eyes flashed again as he turned and opened the door. She flipped off the lights, grabbed her keys, and followed him out. As if already understood, Shane put his hand on her low back while they walked down the stairs to his apartment. Rowan felt his body heat seeping into her system, causing her body to both relax and ramp up at the same time.

Shane opened his door and waited for her to enter. Obviously he was expecting her; the lights were low, there was a bottle of wine breathing on the table, and soft music was playing. Rowan grinned.

"I'm guessing you thought I was a sure thing, huh?" she said.

"No, but a man can dream, and every once in a while, get lucky," he said, his eyebrows rising.

They both laughed. Rowan noticed that she wasn't nervous. Excited yes, but none of the awkwardness she usually experienced with her lovers was present. His apartment was so much nicer than hers. So much more permanent. Heavy bookcases lined the walls and a large TV sat in an entertainment center with stacks of DVD cases and a stereo. His kitchen had an actual table and four chairs. She sat in one of them, grateful of their presence. Maybe she should get some chairs. Even folding chairs might be nice.

Shane poured the wine. As he came close to her, she flashed on the feeling of his hand stroking her thigh. A small shudder eased across her body at the memory. He handed her the glass of wine, watching her as she sipped it. Looking up, she saw something cross his eyes briefly.

"You okay?" she asked, not knowing if that was desire, fear, or something else.

He paused, looked her square in the eye, and laughed uncomfortably. "Yeah. Nothing really gets past you, huh?"

Not sure what that even meant, Rowan just laughed and drank another sip of wine. She felt him watching her again. Never had a man just watched her like he did. Her blood warmed at the thought.

Suddenly too warm under his scrutiny to sit, she stood and started to study the bookshelves. She loved books. That was truly the one thing she missed these last few years, being surrounded by her books.

She could hear him chuckling behind her, but she continued to peruse the titles. Mostly popular mysteries and action paperbacks lined the shelves, but there were some unusual titles as well. *Injuries Children Could Never Acquire Themselves*, and *Trade Secrets of the Best PIs in the Business. Run But You Cannot Hide* gave her a moment's pause.

"That's some nice reading, there. Not too pretty, but great insights into the business." Shane's voice was close. She could feel his hot breath on her neck.

"Yes. I can see that. I think I'd rather read Lee Child than the one about injuries." Rowan laughed a little.

Electricity skidded across her skin as he continued to stand so close to her. Goosebumps broke out across her arms, and her heart fluttered as he laughed deeply behind her.

His hand caressed the back of her head as he pulled her hair off of her neck. She felt his hot lips brush against her soft skin.

With a deep exhale, he told her, "God, Rowan, you are so beautiful. Please tell me this is okay."

Her entire being tightened. Heat flashed up her

body, and just as quickly a shiver wracked her insides. His hot mouth slid up her neck, tiny kisses following all the way back down to her shoulder.

Holding her wine glass so tightly, Rowan was afraid she was going to break it. Her entire body was on fire, waiting for more. Torn between wanting to turn and devour his mouth and wanting him to continue his delicious assault on her neck, she stood motionless, panting.

Slowly, he turned her, kissing her collarbone and neck as she moved in his arms. He took the wine glass out of her hand and set it on the shelf. His five o'clock shadow gently scraped across the delicate skin along her neck as he placed slow, open mouth kisses down to her collarbone.

She opened her eyes to see his, dark and stormy, staring at her, his question lingering in the air. "Yes," she breathed, "Yes, this is okay."

With that he leaned into her, his lips hovering just over hers, waiting. She could feel his breath on her mouth, and with each passing second she wanted him more. No, needed him to kiss her. Finally, she leaned into him, their lips colliding. His lips were soft and warm and she sank into them. When his tongue found its way inside her mouth, her brain felt as if fire works were shooting out of it.

With her hands now free of the useless glass, she ran them up his strong arms, across his shoulders. His muscles were flexing and twitching under her touch. She ran her nails up his neck and drove her fingers into his hair. What little there was of it, the softness with his short cut surprised her. Her fingers felt like they were running though silk.

A low growl from deep within him let loose as his mouth found her breast. With quick hands, he lifted her shirt and pulled it off her head. As his mouth came back down over her lace covered nipple, Rowan shuddered.

Each touch, each kiss, felt as if hot wax was dripping into her veins. Soon her body felt like molten lava. Strong hands smoothed along her thighs and cupped her ass, squeezing. She pushed up on his shoulders and jumped up into him, wrapping her legs around his waist.

The moved seemed to surprise him, and another moan escaped as he took her ass with both hands and carried her away from the forgotten books. Rowan knew they were moving, but didn't care where. She knew only his touch. All other thought, worry, and mantra were blown away. His touch scorched her skin, heating her blood so fast she feared she might combust.

Even while he walked, his magic mouth nipped and kissed her along her neck. His hands kneaded her ass, teasing her like no one had ever done before. He sat her down on the bed and started to toe off his shoes. She unsnapped her bra and slid off her shorts, swallowing hard as he whipped off his shirt, exposing his hard abs and large chest.

Nothing ever looked so tantalizing. His eyes flashed again, that look made her slick between her legs instantly. He paused, panting.

"Jesus," he said under his breath.

Rowan smiled, her eyes dancing. "Yeah. I'm right there."

With that he slammed down on top of her, covering her naked body with his. His hands slid across her skin in long sensual strokes. He continued to kiss her neck, just under her ear, all while his large hands swept up and down her body, running along her hips and ribs, down her legs. Rowan leaned her head back, drowning in the sweet feel of his rough hands.

Shane worked his way down her sides, kissing and running his tongue along her ribs. His hand smoothed along her right side while his mouth worshipped her left. As his mouth kissed the soft part between her ribs and hips, her pelvis flew off the bed, arching toward him. The need she felt was driving her wild.

"Shane," she moaned. "Please. I need you inside of me."

He didn't move, but she felt him smile into her hip as he continued his sweet torture. His right hand glided toward the center of her flat stomach, slowly slipping down. His fingers light, barely brushing across her skin. His mouth, still hot and wet, worked its way down to her center.

"Shane," Rowan cried out with a rough, deep voice, hardly recognizable.

His fingers found the small bit of hair covering her mound. His tongue slid down, meeting up with his hand, as if he planned it that way. Again, her hips thrust up against him, arching, reaching, begging.

"Easy," Shane breathed out, his mouth inches from her sex.

Rowan stilled. Panting, feeling his hand and his breath on her, waiting. Right before she was going to completely lose it, she felt his tongue slide across her. A cry fell out of her and he held her hips steady. Rowan saw stars behind her eyes with his second pass, his tongue dipping inside of her briefly. She growled.

An actual growl erupted from her throat. If Rowan had had her mental facilities, she would have been shocked, but as it was, she didn't even notice. Electric currents were shooting from his tongue up her body, curling her toes and making her scalp tingle. When his mouth settled around her clit, she felt herself vibrating.

Nothing had prepared her for this. She somehow always knew that sex with Shane would be explosive, and even though it had been a long time since she had been with anyone, this was still beyond anything she could've imagined. None of her lovers had ever had her on edge like this. Never had she seen stars, or felt like she was drowning in the sensations of her own body.

"Jesus, Rowan. You taste so fucking good." Shane groaned while flicking his tongue over her clit.

The orgasm that hit was something out of this world. Suddenly, her brain exploded with pleasure while her insides pulsated and flooded. The scream that Rowan heard must have come from her, but she was too far gone to hear it or even register that it came from her throat. It would only be later, when she felt the rawness, that she would know for sure.

• • •

Looking down at the most beautiful and sexy creature Shane had ever seen in his life, his heart squeezed and he almost stopped breathing. She lay there, spread open, wet and panting. Her eyes were glowing hazel. Glowing. He had never seen anything like it before.

His tongue ran over his lips and he could taste the sweetest flavor: her. If he thought her noises and movements were fucking hot before she came on his tongue, afterward there was nothing better. His mind was completely blown, and he hadn't even been inside of her yet.

He needed to be inside of her right now. Stepping back to get a condom was almost painful, he didn't want to take his eyes off her. He still couldn't believe she was there, in his bed, open and waiting for him. A shudder ran through his body as he thought about what was next.

Grinning like a fool, he slipped the condom over his rock hard length and covered her body with his. Rowan arched up to meet him, pushing her perfect breasts into his chest as their bodies met. She wrapped her legs around his waist and pulled him closer.

His cock jerked as he felt the heat of her skin so close to him. His mouth went back to her neck. Oh, that glorious neck, so long and edible. He couldn't get enough of it. Sliding his hand across her body once again, he felt her tremors underneath his fingers all the way down. Reaching into the center of the two of them, he grabbed his cock and positioned himself right at her entrance.

Rowan sighed as her eyes fluttered. He wanted to go slow and enjoy every inch as he sunk into heaven. Watching her and listening to her purr like a cat, he couldn't wait. He needed to be balls deep, right now. He slammed his hips down and drove all the way in.

"Oh!" Rowan's eyes opened wide and she looked shocked.

"Shit. Did I hurt you?" Shane was sweating now, desperately trying to hold back.

"No," she laughed, a throaty laugh that made his cock twitch inside of her. "No. You're just really big."

Shane smiled and kissed her lips. "Oh, baby. You know how to stroke a man's ego."

She slid her tongue along his mouth and sucked on her lower lip. Blackness threatened Shane. He couldn't hold back any more, he needed to move. Drawing out almost his entire length and thrusting back in, her legs opened wider, letting go of his waist.

Breaking free from her kiss, he took his weight on his elbows. Cocooning her head, he ran open mouth kisses down her jaw and neck while his hips took on a life of their own, slamming into her over and over again.

Shane had never felt such sweet pleasure before. She was tight and hot, and completely receptive to him, so damn responsive. When he heard her moan, his eyes went to her face. Feeling as if an angel had landed in his bed, he stilled. Her mouth was open, her eyes closed, and a look of pure ecstasy was on her face.

"No. Don't stop. Don't ever stop," Rowan moaned, spurring him back into action.

His eyes never waivered, he felt her hips moving in small circular motions, meeting his hips, sending him deeper into heaven. With every moan, every breath she took, he felt as if he was traveling through time and space into a place of complete bliss.

"Oh God. Shane. That is so good." Her husky voice broke through his haze and tingles started to fly up and down his spine, settling right at the base, gathering strength.

"You're so beautiful," Shane told her.

Her orgasm was building fast; her breath was hard and heavy, her head shaking from side to side. Shane lost track of the oh gods and yeses that slipped so alluringly out of her sexy mouth. Suddenly, she pressed up on her hands, changing the angle dramatically, and her insides started pulsating. Slick, hot wetness surrounded his cock and he lost it.

He held her stare and unloaded inside of her, praying that the condom could hold it all. Hearing a growl so loud and feral come out of his mouth would have been shocking except for the ecstasy flowing through him. Rowan smiled, a sultry, sexy, vampish smile. And that's when Shane knew.

He knew then that this woman didn't just have secrets; she had layers and layers of secrets. He never expected her to be so open and seductive in bed, he never expected her to steal his heart after just one night. But that was exactly what was happening. He watched, as if he was an outside observer, watched her reach into his chest and take hold of his heart.

She collapsed back down and he followed her. Panting and sweating, he lay unprotected and vulnerable as she stroked his hair. With every stroke, she gathered more of his heart. His eyes fluttered shut. His last thought, before falling into a deep sleep still inside of her, was that this woman owned him.

CHAPTER NINE

Sneaking back into her apartment, trying not to wake up Justin, Rowan slipped into the shower. She had been up for hours waiting for the right moment to leave Shane. He slept soundly next to her, his arm resting on her hip, the sheet covering his lower body. She had stayed there listening to his breathing.

Racked with emotions she had no business having and seemingly out of resources to deal with it all, she feigned sleep, letting her mind wander in and out of fantasy and fear. After several hours she just couldn't take it anymore, so with a whispered good bye to Shane, she snuck out, closing the door to his apartment, and hopefully the door to her heart that had haphazardly opened sometime last night.

She didn't know when exactly, but she knew that something had moved the steel doors she erected the night she walked out on Colt. Having never wanted to experience anything like that again, she was trying not to panic at the thought of a break in the fortress.

Guess now was as good a time to move as any, right? Her job was coming to an end, Justin was here and out of work, so why stay? It made sense to move. Today.

"Morning!" Justin walked into the kitchen and gave her a sheepish smile.

"Morning, Sunshine. What are you so damn happy about?" Rowan grumbled into her coffee.

"Oh! That bad, huh? What happened, he not as good as you hoped?" Justin grabbed a bowl and the cereal.

"Justin Ross. We're so not going there."

He laughed. "Just saying." He wiggled his eyebrows as he went to sit at the cushion that served as a kitchen chair.

She blew out a breath, not wanting to take out her frustration on him. "So, I was thinking it's time to move on. I'm almost done with my summer gig. One more week of full time, if we leave now, it won't be too hard on the girls there."

Justin stopped eating and stared at her. "You want to move? Today?"

"Yeah. I figured we get you settled somewhere, then I could find something for the winter." Rowan sat on the bean bag looking depleted.

Justin was quiet for a minute and then burst into laugher. "Oh my god. He wasn't bad, he was good. Really good, and you're freaking out!"

"God damn it, Justin. We are not discussing my love life." Rowan jumped up, almost spilling her coffee.

"Fine, whatever. But I'm not leaving today. I found work, so I'm sticking around for a while," Justin told her, watching her carefully.

"You found a job?"

"Yeah. And I gotta get to it. So I can't pack." He got up and dumped the contents of his bowl in the sink and washed it down.

She watched as Justin grabbed his keys and walked out without so much as a glance over his shoulder.

Well shit. Now what? Checking the clock, she noted the time; she needed to get to work. Well, not for a few hours, but it was better than sitting here worrying. She could get started on stocking and cleaning. She needed to do something.

She grabbed her keys and stormed out.

• • •

Waking up to an empty bed was not how Shane wanted to start his day. Finding his apartment empty was when his mood plummeted to foul. What the fuck? When did she leave? He knew she was still there at 3 AM, when he woke up and covered her naked body with a sheet. Under the green glow from the clock, her body looked like a nymph tempting him with carnal secrets. He had watched her for a while, holding back the urge to roll her over and delve back into heaven. She was sleeping so peacefully he let her be.

And now she was gone. Gone gone; her apartment was empty; her car was gone. The Snack Shack didn't open for two hours, so where the hell was she? He wondered if she was with Justin. They must have left somewhere together, doing whatever secret things 'relatives' do. He didn't know what was up with those two, but something was.

His phone beeped, making his heart jolt. Grabbing it hoping it was Rowan, he was disappointed when he saw a text from Cody.

"Breakfast. Baker's Square on 3rd. Now."

Shrugging, he decided it was better than moping around here.

~

Pulling into the parking lot, Shane saw both Cody and Rob's trucks. Whatever was up, it was going to be fun, and just what he needed to get his mind to stop spinning.

Walking up, he didn't expect to see Justin sitting at the table, acting like he had nothing better to do than hang out with his two best friends, but there he was, eating breakfast.

"Adams!" Rob called over to him as he slowly approached.

"Hey guys, what's up? Justin." Shane nodded to Justin as he sat down.

Justin just stared at him and slowly nodded back.

"So, here's what's going down. I need back up on a tail. You told me the kid here is good at tailing, so I picked him up earlier when I came by your place. This guy is slippery. It's like he knows we're there and cuts loose. Can't get more than a few hours at a time," Rob started, but Shane wasn't really listening.

He wanted to know where Rowan was. If she wasn't with Justin, than where the hell was she?

"Adams," Rob was calling him. "What the fuck, man?"

"Yeah. No worries. Justin, you see Rowan this morning?" He hadn't shifted his eyes from Justin's since they sat down.

Justin smiled a tight smile. "Yeah man. She's cool. Not getting in the middle of it though, but you can thank me later for keeping her around a little longer."

What? Shane's brain exploded. Keeping her around a little longer? What the hell was he talking about?

"You guys have plans to leave?" Shane asked, his voice tight.

Justin smiled, sitting back, "Not anymore. Told her

this morning I had a job and couldn't pack. That should hold her another week or so. Maybe less. The rest is up to you."

As if that was the end of it, Justin turned his attention back to his food while Shane sat dumbfounded staring at him. Just like Rowan, the kid spoke in riddles, and it was really starting to piss him off.

"Adams!" Rob slapped the table in front of him. "I don't know what the fuck's got your head up your ass, but I'm going to need you fully on board today. You in, or do you need to go suck your dick somewhere?"

Justin snickered. Shane glared at him, then a slow smile spread across his face. Justin really was a kid; he didn't need to get in the middle of whatever was going on between him and Rowan. Relative or not. Not his business.

"Yeah. I'm good." Shane looked at Rob, fully engaged.

• • •

One more week. Rowan climbed the stairs to her apartment, exhausted after having spent yet another day behind the grill. The pool had one more weekend, then Labor Day would lead right into back to school. She had fond memories of back to school week. All the kids coming back in from their summers with their parents: Their hair long and dirty, their clothes full of holes and worn, their bodies in need of consistent nourishment and sleep.

Even Justin was out of routine by then. It always took everyone, herself included, some time to get back into it, but within a few weeks everyone would have settled down for a nice long winter, secluded and protected from the rest of their world.

She could do one more week with the grease and the girls. They were constantly getting into dramas with their friends and parents. A few even had boyfriend dramas to entertain her as the days flew by. She would miss those girls; hearing their stories always made her laugh. Today, Tami had been telling her all about how she and her sister both liked the same boy, and he seemed to like them both back equally. Rowan did what she always did, she listened and advised that family, real family, was worth more than some guy. Even a guy that seemed like a great, wonderful, trustworthy person. Never let a guy get in the way of family.

Pulling off her clothes and stuffing them into a large plastic garbage bag, she jumped into the shower. The warm water reminded her of last night. Shane. What a mistake to go to bed with him. Never in a millions years did she think it would be like that. She thought it would just be another roll in the hay—all the other ones were just that, nothing more. Sure, some of them had wanted more than one night, and she usually stuck around for a while, but they had been easy to leave behind. Shane was different.

Shane had the power to take her down. She knew that was the reason she couldn't sleep. She had realized that he just might hold the power to ruin her, and she vowed never to let that happen again. Even if she needed to run from two people, she would, she knew running. Running was better than being ripped apart by another person's weakness. Never. Never again.

"Ro?" Justin called her name as she stepped out of the bathroom.

"Yeah baby, what's up?" Rowan peeked her head around the corner, still in her towel, and stopped short.

Both Shane and Justin were standing in the living room. Shane's face was full of fury and before she could say anything he turned and walked out.

"Baby?" Justin asked, with a smirk on his face. "Feeling nostalgic, are we?"

Rowan just stood there, stunned. That look on Shane's face was more than she could bear. No, she didn't want Shane to break her, but she never wanted to hurt him. Now she was going to have to go over there and explain this whole thing to him. Damn it. So much for just avoiding him.

"Yeah. I was. It was short lived," Rowan clipped back at him and marched down the hall to get dressed.

When she came back out, Justin was reading in the living room. "You going to go tell your boyfriend I'm not a threat to him?" he deadpanned.

"He's not my boyfriend. And yes, thanks to you, I'm going to have to tell him something," she said as she gathered up Justin's laundry.

"Well, just so you know. I'm cool with it. It's just better if people know. Besides. I'm not ashamed of it." Justin stared at her, hard.

"Justin. I'm not ashamed of it. I just think people won't understand the circumstances, and it's too exhausting to explain. People don't need to know our business," She told him, still gathering scattered clothes and cleaning up the room.

"Yeah, whatever Ro. You're the boss."

She felt the cut, but didn't take the bait. They'd been over this, and they were not getting into it again. She had too many balls in the air already. Justin was just going to have to take his adolescent, sarcastic self elsewhere.

Satisfied with the laundry pile and the state of the living room, she turned to leave. As she got to the door, Justin turned on the radio and cranked the volume, Rowan shut it behind her and headed downstairs.

With a bitter taste in her mouth, she looked over at Shane's apartment. The windows were covered, but light was glowing behind the curtains and music was leaking out of the doors and walls. Great, now two men were so royally pissed at her that they were both holed up in their apartments, about to get in trouble with their neighbors.

How the hell did this day get so bad? Not 24 hours ago life was easy and exciting—she needed to fix things with both Shane and Justin. At 18, Justin was a hard nut to crack, but she hoped Shane would be easy. She would start with Shane and work up to Justin.

Pounding on his door for what felt like the tenth time, the music finally faded enough, so she called out his name.

"Shane. It's Rowan. Let me in."

The door swung open to a shirtless Shane with an open beer.

"Hey baby," Shane sneered at her.

Rowan pushed herself in. "Oh, please. Get over yourself."

"Come on in, why don't cha'," Shane said with the same caustic tone.

"First of all, Justin is a baby. He's 18 years old, and if you think for one goddamn minute that I would be with someone that young, you're sick and need your head checked." Rowan glared at him.

Shane's head snapped up to her, his eyes wide with surprise.

"Second. I call him baby because I have known him

a long, long time. So if you can't handle that I have a caring, loving, normal relationship with a close relative, then I can walk out right now. Got it?" She continued.

"Yeah. I got it." He blew out a breath as a smile played around his lips.

"Good." Rowan nodded and headed for the door again.

"Where're you going?" He blocked her way and glared at her.

"I need to go now," she stuttered, not looking at him in the eye.

"The fuck you are!" He roared over her. "You can't just leave. Where the hell were you this morning?"

Rowan paused and took a deep breath. That was her first mistake. His scent filled her brain, overwhelming her senses, making her swoon a little on her feet. Putting on a brave face, she looked up at him. That was her second mistake. Her eyes took in his bare, muscled chest and her mouth started to water. His eyes looked hurt and scared as he stared at her, waiting for his answer.

"I had—I had to go to work," She weakly lied to him.

Something flashed in his eyes and she knew he caught the lie. Was that disappointment?

"Work? At 6 am?" he asked her, holding her eyes steady.

"Um. Well, I had to run before it got too hot," she tried again. This time, his eyes narrowed.

"So did you? Run?" he clipped.

She looked down, not able to take his scrutiny anymore. Her body was being pulled into him while her brain was screaming for her to get out. It was an exhausting battle, and she couldn't fight herself and

Shane at the same time. Defeated, she stepped back and let out a long breath.

He reached for her and she crumbled. He wrapped his strong arms around her and pulled her tight against him. She felt like a little piece of heaven was just offered to her, and she held on with everything she had. She breathed in his masculine scent and for the first time in a long while, she let herself be comforted by a robust man. It was intoxicating.

"Tell me what happened?" Shane whispered.

Not knowing what to say or do, she felt weak, as if pushing Shane away was physically unattainable. She wanted nothing more than to curl up in his arms and sleep. She was so tired. And so confused; all her resolve to stay away from him had just evaporated into nothing.

Looking up at him, her eyes watery from the toll of the day, she held his gaze. His hand cupped her face and she leaned into his touch. So weak, she couldn't hold back; when he brushed his lips gently over hers, almost asking for permission, she had no choice but to lean into his mouth and kiss him back.

As if the keystone to his restraint was torn down, he plundered her mouth. His hands smoothed down her hips, sliding across to her backside, pressing her into his already hard and waiting body. He moaned as she rubbed herself on him, moving her legs so her sex was sitting on his thigh.

Pulling her hair, he forced her head to tip back, opening her throat for him. Shane ravished her neck as shivers ran across her skin. Sounding as if it was being ripped involuntarily from her, a moan rang out into the room.

"Oh God, Rowan. I thought you were gone." He moaned into her skin, igniting her blood and need. He pulled at her clothes, tugging off her shorts with a desperation she didn't know he possessed.

She knew she shouldn't feel so good about this. This wasn't happening; she was gone—moving away from him—at least, she needed to be, but right now hearing his voice, feeling his touch, she relished it. Her body became alive with his anguish. Having stripped her of her shorts, he picked her up and slammed her into the wall.

"Fuck," Shane muttered, setting her back down. He stripped off his jeans and ran to get a condom, pulling it over his hard cock while walking back to her. Rowan watched from her place near the wall, her body screaming for him. He grinned lasciviously as he stalked toward her, hard, sheathed, ready to devour his prey.

Picking her up again, he leaned her back against the wall for support. He braced her there while coming up underneath her slowly, bringing her down on top of him. The cold wall collided with his scorching heat, stopping her breath. Rowan slammed her head back, moaning. With every inch they were joined, she died and went to a better and better heaven.

When he was completely inside her, he stilled. Her clit throbbed and her insides started to convulse around him. She needed more.

"Shane," she growled at him, opening her eyes and drinking him in. "Fuck me. Please."

She watched as Shane's eyes dilated with desire, then she felt his first thrust. A piercing cry of ecstasy filled the apartment. Shane's or Rowan's, she didn't know or care. His head was down and he was grunting with each hard thrust. Her hips and head slammed into the wall over and over again. She'd never felt anything better. Tingles and currents moved throughout her body, the pressure building up inside of her so intense she thought she might explode.

The pain mixed with pleasure was something so new she felt giddy experiencing it. Never had any of her lovers taken her against a wall. She felt like she could light the world. If she touched an electric socket she would burn it out. Her toes curled, her breasts tightened, and another growl escaped her mouth as if a wild animal was trying to get out. Tingles from her clit started moving down her legs, each thrust making it stronger and stronger. Oh, the promise of her orgasm was right there. So close, the pleasure was so intense she thought her mind would snap.

"Shane. Oh God, Shane. Don't stop," she sobbed with stars in her eyes. When her orgasm took over her body she screamed his name, her body wracked by sobs.

"Fuck, Rowan," Shane roared as he came inside of her. She was barely aware of it, her orgasm was so powerful.

He thrust into her a few more times then stilled. They leaned against each other and the wall, the apartment quiet except for their panting. Slowly, her legs slipped down his body and met the floor. Still shaky, she waited for him to disconnect from her.

When he slowly walked away to take care of the condom, she took a small step and collapsed into the nearest chair. She didn't know what to do or what to think. In fact, thinking was out of the question; she sat, her mind filled with nothing.

He reached for her and she stood. Following him to the shower, she stepped into the hot water and let him wash her. He lovingly massaged soap all over her body then washed it off with warm water. She tried to soap him too, but her arms wouldn't move.

He smiled and took the soap out of her hand, washing himself.

After the shower he wrapped her in a towel and led her to his bed. Slipping into the sheets, the last thing she heard was Shane whispering in her ear, "Please be here in the morning."

CHAPTER TEN

Shane awoke to the phone vibrating on the table. Rowan's body was pressed into him and he really didn't want to move, but he knew that only a few people called him at this hour, and only if they needed him.

"Yo," he answered, trying hard not to sound pissed and asleep.

"It's happening. Now. Get the kid." Cody's voice was tight.

"Yep. Be there in ten." Shane put the phone down and started extracting himself from Rowan.

"Where are you sneaking off to?" Rowan's sleepy voice floated up from her pillow.

"I gotta go. I'll be back. Please be here when I get back. It's just work." He leaned over and kissed her head, breathing in her scent.

"Yeah. Don't be too long," Rowan mumbled and resettled into the bed.

Shane dressed and grabbed his gear. He was out the door in less than three minutes and up the stairs pounding on Justin's door in four.

"Justin. Get up. It's Shane."

Just then, the door opened. Justin was dressed, his

hand wrapped around the grip of a gun he had tucked into the waist of his jeans.

"Jesus kid. What the hell?"

"Just habit. What's up? Rowan okay?" Justin asked, running a hand through his hair.

"She's fine. Cody called. Rob needs back up. Now." Shane looked around the apartment. Something seemed off, but he couldn't place it and they needed to go.

"Right. Hold on." Justin turned to the back bedroom.

Shane tried to wake up while Justin was gone. He looked around the apartment again, then the smell hit him. Scented candles. Holy shit. Justin had a date! Sure enough, he heard voices from the back. Hiding his smile, he waited for Justin to reappear.

"Okay. Let's move," Justin said as he came out of the bedroom.

"Okay, Romeo. Let's go." Shane chuckled as he turned around to walk out. He heard Justin mutter a curse as he closed and locked the door.

"Should I go tell Rowan to stay out, lest she walk in on that?" Shane asked him, smiling.

"Just don't, okay. I'm hoping to be back before she gets up." Justin sounded so serious that he took pity on him and let it go.

Five minutes later, Shane pulled out of the parking lot with Justin in the passenger seat.

"So, I think I owe you one." Shane spoke quietly.

Justin's head whipped up. "Why?" he asked, suspiciously.

"Man! What is with you two? Because you said you kept her around. So, thanks." Shane focused on the road ahead of him.

"Yeah. No worries. Did she tell you? Ya know,

about me." Justin seemed nervous, piquing Shane's curiosity yet again.

"Yeah. She said you guys go way back. Known each other for a long time. It's all good." Shane watched him out of the corner of his eye while he spoke and noticed Justin's jaw clench down.

Shane's eyes went back to the road and Justin blew out a breath. Shane turned back to look at him again, but he just smiled tightly and nodded. Okay, so there was obviously more to the story there. Justin was not pleased and wasn't hiding it well.

They drove a few more minutes before turning down a dirt alley and parking. Shane reached under his seat and pulled out his Glock 9, checking to see if it was fully loaded and that the safety was off. He looked over at Justin and to his surprise he was doing the same thing.

"Nice piece, kid. Where the hell did you get that?" Shane was impressed to see him sitting there with a fully loaded Colt M1911.

Justin checked the safety and looked up at him, smiling. "Oh, this? From Rowan. For my 15th birthday. That was a killer party. Don't worry, I know what I'm doing." His eyes flashed with smugness and he jumped out of the car.

What. The. Fuck?

"You coming?" Justin called through the window.

He snapped out of it and opened his door.

They met Cody and Rob around the corner. Cody looked like he was having the time of his life. All smiles, cracking jokes. Rob, on the other hand, looked like he could snap at any moment.

"Alright. This is what I got. Been trying to get into that house for three weeks. He has a back room that shows a lot of activity on the infrared, but so far only two people have come and gone. They're hauling in a lot of something. I'm thinking more girls, or something worse. For some reason tonight they both left and came back after about an hour. They've been drinking. The one guy was stumbling drunk and his buddy dropped him off then left. He's in there passed out, and the other guy is definitely at a booty call." Rob laid it out.

"Okay," Justin piped up. "I'll go in and check the back room. You two cover me, and you better fucking make some noise if he wakes up or his buddy comes back."

"What? No way you're going in," Shane almost shouted.

"No dude. He got this. This dude knows his shit. He moves like a fucking ninja," Cody whispered to Shane.

"What the fuck you guys been doing with him? He's a fucking kid!" Shane asked, incredulously.

Justin snorted. "I'm not a kid, and I've been doing this shit for years. Relax." Justin pulled out his gun and checked it one more time.

Shane watched in awe as Justin moved out, gun in hand, creeping over the grass. They were right, he moved fast, and he was silent. They waited until he was at the house and then they moved forward as a group. Much slower and with a lot more noise than Justin the Ninja.

"The kid knows what's up. I told you. Never seen anyone move like that," Cody whispered to him.

Shane moved close to the house and pressed his ear to the wall. Nothing. Where the hell did he go? He tensed, every sense alive, waiting. Creeping along the wall to the front, he hoped to see inside. Hearing no movement at all in the house, he wondered if maybe Justin hadn't make it inside yet.

"Hey, Shane!" Justin's whisper-shout gave Shane a

heart attack. "It's a fucking pot farm. No girls. Go get Rob, what does he want me to do?"

Justin was standing on the front porch. Jesus. Cody was right, the kid was a ninja. How in the hell did he do that? Shane nodded and turned back to find Rob. Shane found him at the back door, waiting for Justin.

"Rob, he's at the front. Says it's a pot farm. What do you want to do?" Shane whispered to him.

Rob turned toward him. "He's at the front?"

"Yeah. Walked out the fucking front door." Shane smiled. He couldn't help but be impressed.

"A pot farm? Three fucking weeks for a goddamn pot farm?" Rob stood up and started walking toward the front.

Cody joined them as they rounded the corner.

"Oh shit." Cody started running.

Shane looked up and saw a man walk up the porch. As he reached for the front door, Justin came out nowhere and put the gun right in his face. He was eerily calm; obviously this wasn't the first time he had pulled a gun on someone. He knew exactly what he was doing.

Shane ran toward them.

"What the fuck, man? You here to rip me off? You're fucking dead," The man shouted.

Before Shane or Cody could get there, Justin had him on the ground in a wrist hold, pressing the gun in the side of his head.

"No, man. I'm not here to rip you off. I'm looking for a friend of mine. This isn't his house, man. So you're going to calm the fuck down, and I'm going to go find my friend." Justin wasn't even breathing heavy when he spoke to him.

The man was struggling against him, but Justin had him subdued, there wasn't a thing he could do. When

Justin looked over at Rob he just shook his head, and the three of them started backing away.

"So listen, man. I'm going to let you go and you're going to go in your fucking house and I'm going to go find my friend? You got that, man?" Justin spoke, emphasizing 'man'.

"Fuck you, man! No one comes into my house and fucks with me, you piece of shit," The guy on the ground shouted.

Shane started moving back to Justin and the commotion, but Justin looked up at him and shook his head again, smiling.

"Okay, man. You asked for it," Justin said, looking at Shane.

Shane watched as Justin put his gun down and moved his hand over the guy's neck. After a minute or so Justin got up, slipped his gun into his pants, and walked over to him.

"What the hell did you do?" Shane asked before he even reached him.

"Just knocked him out. He'll be fine," Justin said, walking past him.

Following him, he wondered who in the hell this guy was, and what the hell he was to Rowan. When they got back to the cars, Justin calmly adjusted his gun and waited, standing near the Kia.

"Well, that blows," Rob said as he opened his car.

"No worries, man. What were you looking for, anyway?" Cody asked him.

"Wasn't sure. The intel was vague. Just was hired to follow him and find out what he was doing. The whole thing was strange. But in this business, what isn't, right?" Rob said as he slid into his truck.

"Okay. See you later," Shane called over his shoulder as he walked to his car.

Justin followed, silently. Shane had all kinds of questions for him, but he kept his mouth shut. He couldn't figure what he wanted to know first. Rowan gave him a Colt M1911 for his 15th birthday? How does an 18 year old acquire skills like that? Shane had been in the business for years and was just getting comfortable confronting people. And they way he moved in that house, it was like he was born for it.

They drove back without speaking. He had no idea what Justin was thinking, the kid was like a tomb, just like Rowan. They were a lot alike that way. When they wanted to shut down their emotions they just locked up. He wondered what other connections they had, in fact, he wanted to know what their real connection was.

Shane pulled in and parked, letting the engine run. He turned to Justin and opened his mouth to speak.

"Nope. I'm not even going there with you. You got questions, you ask Rowan." Justin spoke first, then opened his door and jumped out.

He was halfway up the stairs before Shane was even out of his car. He watched as Justin slipped into the apartment, then he turned and walked into his own, where Rowan was hopefully still waiting for him.

• • •

Rowan awoke to the smell of coffee and clean sheets. She stretched and opened her eyes. Her body felt like it was floating. Not only had she had amazing sex, but she'd slept in a real bed for the first time in almost two years. Oh, the luxury of it all. She couldn't hide the grin on her face.

Shane walked in with two coffee cups and she groaned.

"Hmmm. You make more noises like that, your coffee will be cold by the time you get to it." His voice was low and full of promise.

"Oh, God. This is the most comfortable bed I've ever slept in," she said without moving.

Sitting down, he leaned over her, "So it's really all about the bed, is it?"

Looking up at him, his eyes were sparkling and she could tell he was teasing, so she laughed and rolled away from him.

"And the coffee. I really love coffee," she said, smiling.

"God, you're beautiful," Shane spoke with a reverence not foreign to her.

Her eyes flew open and connected with his. His mouth was slightly open, and his eyes went back to roaming her body. She watched him lick his lips as his eyes slowly moved up, finally meeting hers. He reached out and gently placed his hand on her neck, slowly moving down her shoulder to her hip. When he started to move his hand back up her body across her stomach, she sat up and scooted away from him.

Reaching for her coffee, she pulled the sheet around herself. It was getting a little too serious for her. That look, she had seen that look before, and it never ended well.

"Um, I think I need to go home now." She smiled as she spoke, hoping to let him off easy.

Stopping, he watched her, tilting his head as if trying to work something out.

"Okay Rowan. But here's the thing. We're not done. Not even close. No bolting, no packing. Don't even think about it." He spoke to her while pinning her with his eyes.

Rowan's eyes flashed in surprise. Goddamn Justin.

When did they even talk to each other? She looked down and felt the panic flood her veins. Sipping her coffee, looking anywhere but at Shane, she took a moment to steady her breath.

"Yeah, well. No promises. I'm looking for work now. So where ever it takes me, I go." She moved off the bed to get up.

Feeling his eyes on her while she got up, she walked to the bathroom, picking up her clothes on the way. Once inside she let the panic take over. Goddamn Justin! Why would he tell him that she wanted to leave? And when? When were they even together? And why? Justin never said a thing to her.

She dressed as quickly as she could. She needed to get home and talk to him. She slipped on her shorts and ran a hand through her hair. So much for her good mood. And she really enjoyed last night. Darn it. She had been really happy, and now — well, now it was time to leave.

When she opened the door to find Shane waiting for her just on the other side, she let out a yelp and held the doorframe.

"Jesus, Shane. You scared the crap out of me," she said, walking through the door.

"Rowan," he gently grabbed her hand and pulled her back to him, "I can see that brain of yours churning. I don't know why you're running, but know this, I can find you."

Rowan stopped breathing. Her breath was lodged into her throat. *He knows I'm running? Wait, he's talking about us.* She let out her breath and started to laugh a little. Shane was watching her as the panic gripped her body and then subsided. His eyes narrowed at her reaction.

Shane pressed her against the wall, caging her in

with his arms. "I don't care how we do this, Rowan. Fast or slow. Run, don't run. Doesn't matter. I'm in. You're in. We can do this any way you want. We can sleep together, we can date, we can move in together. It doesn't matter. This," he gestured between the two of them, "This is happening."

Rowan didn't know what to say. She could barely comprehend the words he had just said. All she knew was that she had to leave before her head exploded.

Hysterical laughter rose from deep inside of her, with it the panic she thought she'd quelled earlier. With no other option, she kissed him lightly on the lips and tried her best to stifle it.

Shane crossed his arms over his chest and watched her closely. Rowan couldn't speak, just maniacally giggles as she walked through the apartment to the front door. She walked up the steps still laughing, still trying to hold the panic at bay. At the top of the stairs she opened her door, and all the panic and laughter died instantly.

CHAPTER ELEVEN

The woman standing in her kitchen was barely dressed, well, not even dressed. She was wearing Justin's shirt with no underwear and her tongue was down his throat. *What the hell is going on?* Rowan cleared her throat.

"Oh shit," Justin said as he noticed Rowan standing in the doorway.

The woman turned around and had the audacity to grin. As if she was claiming him in front of her. That was so wrong.

"Justin. Would you like to introduce me to your houseguest?" Rowan clipped while closing the door.

He locked eyes with her for a second then smiled a tight smile, all while his jaw tensed. "Yeah. Rowan, this is Angie. Angie, this is Rowan. My roommate. We go way back."

She heard the hurt in his voice. Angie seemed to have missed it as she giggled and nodded to her.

"Nice to meet you, Angie. Do you mind putting on some pants? I'd like to make breakfast." Rowan's eyes never left Justin's.

"Sure." Angie giggled again and walked down the hall into the bedroom.

Rowan watched Justin while he nodded to Angie, watching her walk down the hall with a slightly dreamy look in his eyes. Not what Rowan needed to see.

"Way back? Is that how we're doing it now?" Rowan asked as soon as Angie was safely in the back.

"Just following your lead, Ro," Justin clipped back at her defiantly.

That's what she had told Shane — last night, how did Justin find out? And then it dawned on her.

"You went out with Shane last night? You're working with him? Are you crazy?" Her voice was rising. Of course, this was the work he found. Damn it.

"Yep. Shane and I are good buddies these days. No thanks to you," He spoke again, anger dripping off his words.

"And you told him I was packing, didn't you. You told him I wanted to move. That's how he knew. God damn it, Justin. What's up with you? Since when do you work as a PI? Since when do you tell people our business?" Rowan was shouting now. Her entire world was tilting — again.

"Our business. You say that like it's a bad thing. Am I so bad?" The hurt in Justin's voice was devastating. It sliced her open.

"No Justin, you're not bad. It's just me. It's all me. I'm sorry." Rowan spoke quietly, wanting nothing more than to walk across the kitchen and hold him.

Justin took a breath and waited. She knew that look; he had shut down, and she would have to wait to finish this conversation.

"Do you really think it's wise to work with a PI?" She tried a different tactic.

Justin laughed. "Just trying to put my years of

experience to work. Ya know, Jewel always said I was one of the best."

With the mention of Jewel's name, her blood boiled. "So that's what you've been doing? Proving Jewel right?"

Rowan turned and stormed toward the back. She ran into Angie in the hall and slammed her door shut.

"Rowan. That's not what I meant." She heard Justin say behind her.

She was too upset to answer him. Not with Angie in the house and Shane on her mind.

~

The day had gone from shitty to completely wrecked. Work was slow and painful. The girls were all fretting about school and what was going to happen. She tried to engage, but with everything else going on, she just couldn't get worked up about what to wear the first day of high school.

Rowan opened her mailbox feeling beat down and almost dead. The postcard that fell out sent a jolt of adrenaline into her bloodstream immediately. "Let's meet. Lina." Short and simple. But how did she even know where to send the postcard? Rowan ran upstairs to find Justin. Maybe he would know.

Her apartment was empty when she got inside. Darn. She needed to talk to him. Or Talia. Maybe she got it from Talia. First, Rowan needed a shower, then she would call Talia, it would be good to talk to her anyway.

Twenty minutes later, Rowan ran out of the house, having showered, and started a new load of laundry. Given how amped up she was, she walked to the payphone around the corner. So many things were running through her head, she could barely keep them all straight. Justin was sleeping with someone. She knew that was going to happen, but still. That was a shock. Shane was on some romantic kick, and now Lina wanted to meet. She had probably heard the rumors and was hurt. Or maybe this was a trap.

The phone rang twice before Talia answered.

"Talia," Rowan breathed out when she heard her sister's voice. All the emotion she had been trying to hide came flooding back. Talia was her big sister and always did her best to take care of her. Rowan remembered how alone she'd felt when she first left.

"Oh! What's wrong?" Talia's sharp voice pulled her back to the moment.

"Nothing. Everything's fine. Everyone is here. All good," Rowan told her.

They had learned to not use names whenever possible. Just in case. They never knew how serious Jolly was. Rowan knew Jolly was serious and evil. He enjoyed toying with people and never tired of other people's misery.

"Good. What's up?" Talia asked, her voice much more relaxed.

"Just got word from a friend. Wasn't sure how. You know anything about it?" Rowan asked, hoping her sister would know whom she was talking about.

For a few seconds she was silent, then she let out a long breath. "Yes. She came here. Came here to see you. Thought you would be here. It seemed legit. So, I gave her the address. I really hope that was the right choice." Talia sounded tense.

"So far. How do I get word back?" Rowan asked, going with her gut on this one; she couldn't imagine Lina setting a trap. But then, she wouldn't have thought that Colt would leave her high and dry that night, either.

"Just tell me when and where and I'll be the go between. And listen. Stay awake on this one. I feel like it's real, but be ready." Talia sounded so earnest.

Rowan laughed at the 'awake' comment. Using inside lingo seemed funny to her. But still, the message was loud and clear: Always keep your guard up.

"I hear you. Soon?" Rowan asked.

"Yeah, this week. I think she must be out and about. She sounded really excited to find out you were in California. I think she is, too," Talia answered, then spoke to someone in the same room.

Rowan thought hard about where to go. She wanted to see her, but not at the house. And not where Shane could see her. This had to be done right. The least likely place that Shane would be is a fancy hotel.

"Let's meet at the Sheraton Teahouse. Downtown. Tuesday. 2 PM."

"I'll pass it along. Tell him we miss him and he can come back when he wants. He didn't have to leave, ya know. We never would have kicked him out." Talia sounded almost sad now.

"No. He needed to be the cautious adventurer, he's just not so cautious these days." Rowan laughed.

"Okay. Thanks baby. Take care." Talia hung up.

Rowan hung up and wiped a tear from her eyes. Why did they have to live this way? Why the hell did it come to this? She just wanted her family together and to be left alone. She knew that would never happen, but that didn't stop her from wanting it.

Rowan started to head back, but froze when she felt like she was being watched. Scanning the area, she saw a dark blue Kia pulling away. She couldn't be sure, but that looked a lot like Shane's car.

• • •

Watching Rowan wipe tears away from her eyes and looking so longingly at the phone was hard. It was clear she loved whoever she was talking to, and missed them terribly. It didn't help that Justin was with him when he saw her. Shane would have loved to follow her and see what she did next, but that seemed a little creepy with her cousin, or whatever the fuck he was to her, sitting next to him.

"Dude," Justin said.

Shane pulled out and continued driving. They had a job to do and it wasn't going to be fun. This time they needed to sneak, yes, sneak, into an office and retrieve some evidence. The plan was for Shane to distract the front office clerk and let Ninja Boy do his thing.

Shane blew out a breath. "What's the deal with you two? You guys grow up together?"

Justin sat next to him, not moving, not talking.

"Fine, whatever." Shane's anger got the best of him and he slammed the accelerator hard.

"If it was up to me, you'd already know. But it's not. None of this shit was ever up to me," Justin told him, staring out the window.

That got Shane's attention. He focused back on Justin.

"Okay," he said slowly.

Justin blew out a long breath. "Look, there's a lot more going on than Rowan will ever let on. Just be careful with her. She's been hurt. A lot. Even I know that. I don't know everything, but I've done the math. It's fucked up. That's all I can say right now."

Shane was even more confused and intrigued. On one hand, he was elated because he knew something was up with these two, but on the other hand, he had no idea what Justin was talking about. It wasn't a puzzle he was going to figure out on his own. He needed Rowan to open up to him.

"Yeah, okay. I really like her. Like, I'm really into her and I don't want to hurt her. I'm just trying to understand what's going on with her. I'm not going to mess with her head or anything." Shane could hear the desperation in his voice and he didn't like it.

Justin never looked at him, never took his eyes off the road ahead. His jaw tensed a few times, then he said, "You'll never understand, dude. It's unfucking comprehensible."

Shane took that in. What the hell happened to her? To the kid sitting next to him? His urge to dig deeper was overwhelming; he needed to find out the mystery of this woman more than he needed his next breath. He didn't know what Justin was playing at, but all it did was fire him up like nothing ever had. If ever he had a case he wanted to crack, it was this one.

They pulled into the parking lot of Sunshine Marketing a few minutes later. Justin still seemed tense and he needed to get him to relax. If they walked in this wound up they would be called out in a second.

"Hey, Ninja Boy. You okay there?" Shane grabbed his shoulders and shook him.

That seemed to get Justin to snap out of it. He turned and smiled at Shane, shaking his head a little.

"Yeah. Yeah. I got this." Justin smirked. *Good, he was back.*

They walked in together and quickly spilt up. Shane walked over to the front desk lady and sighed in relief to discover she was a young woman with dark hair and an off the shoulder dress. A little dressed up for a receptionist, but it would work to his advantage.

Smiling as he approached, eyes already slightly hooded, he would play this out for as long as he could.

She looked up and paused, watching him, "How can I help you, sir?" Her voice was high and sweet.

"Sir?" he asked, pretending to be wounded. "Do I look that old these days?"

"Oh." She seemed generally shocked at his reaction. "No. I didn't mean old. I was just. Just. I don't know. I call everybody Sir." She floundered in front of him.

"Everybody?" He cocked his head and raised one eyebrow. Laying it on thick.

"Um. Well, no. Not everybody. Just the men. Um. Can I help you?" She was bright red and flustered. Exactly what he was hoping for.

"It's okay. I'm just messing with you. I'm hoping you can help me though," he said, stalling for more time.

She looked at him without speaking. She was cute, big brown eyes, full lips, high cheekbones. Her hair was shoulder length and had a soft wave to it. Now that she wasn't quite so embarrassed, he could see that she was a knockout.

"How can I help you, then?" she asked, with much more composure than before. Shane was impressed.

"Well first, are you single?" he asked her, with an appreciative look in his eye.

Watching her as her brain registered the question, he smiled inwardly. Her mouth opened and shut quickly as her eyes darted around the room and landed back on Shane. He waited while she got her thoughts together.

"I'm really not sure I can answer that question, Sir." She pinned him with a stern look.

Okay, time was running out. Justin had better hurry up and grab that file.

"Sorry. Didn't mean to offend you. It's just you sort of blew me away when I first walked up. I sincerely apologize for being inappropriate." Shane waited for his apology to sink in, giving himself even more time.

This time, a slow blush started just under her neck and worked its way up her face before she could speak. She closed her eyes for a full two seconds before opening them again. And that was all the time he needed. Justin came out and slipped out the door while she was wishing the floor would open up and swallow her.

"You know what," she said, still red, but with clear eyes, "Can we just start over? Please."

"I'll do you one better. I'm going to leave now. Don't worry. I'll come back and we can pretend we've never met. How's that sound?" Shane pulled away from her desk and started to back up.

"That would be great," she said on an exhale.

"Take care." He winked at her as he turned and headed out the building.

Opening the door, he saw two figures near his car. Shit. Someone was confronting Justin. Shane started to run toward his car when he saw the stranger throw a punch. Justin moved lightening fast out of his way. Before he reached them, Justin had the guy leaning over his car hood with his arms pinned behind him. All while still holding the file in one hand. Who the hell was this kid? The next Jason Bourne?

"Like I said. I'm waiting for a friend. Looks like he just got here, and now we're leaving. Thanks for the entertainment. I hate being bored," Justin was saying when Shane got within earshot.

"Hey," Shane said, "Problem?"

"Nope. Right, asshole? We got no problems here,"

Justin answered him in the guy's ear, tightening his grip on his handhold.

"No problems. I was just leaving," The guy said, facedown against the hood.

Justin let him up and stepped back, handing the file to Shane. He slipped it in his jacket before the guy turned around. He glanced a quick look at Shane and then at Justin before storming off.

Shane looked at Justin, questioningly, then opened the car. They both slipped in and he drove back out on the road.

"It's all there. Memos, emails, even an invoice. These guys hired him to sue. It's all in the file," Justin told him as they drove away.

"And the guy in the parking lot?"

"Not a fucking clue. He didn't like me and didn't like that I was holding a file. I'm guessing really bad security," Justin answered him matter of factly.

"Yeah, okay. Good."

CHAPTER TWELVE

Fast or slow. Whatever I want. Isn't that what Shane had told her? Whatever she wanted. He was in, no matter what? He'd seemed so genuine and so unbelievably confident about them. Rowan went over the conversation repeatedly, trying to piece out the words, trying to make them mean something different, but in the end it seemed that Shane was just a nice guy who was really into her. He didn't know anything about her past.

At least, he didn't know anything Justin hadn't told him. She knew Justin meant well, but that had been a blow. She forgot how impulsive teenagers could be. He shouldn't be here with her, it was too dangerous; he needed to be living a regular life, dating girls and flipping burgers for a living, taking a few college classes and getting drunk with his friends. She needed to send him back to Talia's. It was too dangerous for both of them. If he kept this up they'd find her, and if they found her, they'd take him back, too. Jolly didn't want Talia, he gave up on her years ago — Justin would be safe with her.

And now he's working with the PIs. Staying out late and doing god knows what. She supposed it was better than what would have happened to him, but still it felt a little like failure—like she didn't get him out in time. They still corrupted him; he knows too much now. It feels normal to him.

Rowan had been thinking and pacing her apartment for about an hour, waiting for Justin to come home. Her phone call with Talia had been both good and bad, but this wasn't about her anymore. She needed to focus on Justin and get him back to a normal 18 year old life.

She wasn't even sure she should tell him about Lina. She'd been so wrapped up in Shane, she almost forgot all about the meeting. No, she wasn't going to tell Justin about it. She needed Justin to believe she was fine. Fine enough to date a PI, even! That was a good idea, Justin would see she was fine and dating a good man, and then he would go back to Talia's and go to college.

Dating Shane wouldn't be horrible. Her skin shivered thinking about it. He really was a great guy. And sexy. And really good in bed. Small earthquakes shook her body with the memories of the last few nights. And there was something about the way he made her feel that was addictive. When he held her and looked in her eyes, she felt as if she was the only woman alive. He made her feel sexy and cherished. That can't be a bad thing, right?

Rowan heard keys jingling at the door. Justin was finally home. The door opened and Rowan started walking toward it.

"Justin. I'm really sorry about—" Rowan stopped speaking when she looked up and saw Shane standing in the doorway.

Justin walked in and gestured to Shane to follow. Shane's eyes locked with hers and she felt every nerve come alive and start pulsing, the heat in Shane's eyes speaking to her on a cellular level. She wasn't strong enough to deny it. She wanted this as much as he did.

"You were saying?" Justin broke the silence.

Rowan looked over at him to see him grinning at her.

"What?" Rowan couldn't remember what she had been saying. It was something, but for the life of her she couldn't think of it.

Justin laughed out loud. "Jesus, Ro. Whatever. Don't worry about it. I got the message. You're sorry for being PMSy this morning and you love me. I know." Justin laughed as he walked down the hall.

Rowan snapped out of it. "Wait a minute, Mister." She turned to Shane. "Was he working with you today?"

Shane's eyes widened in surprise. "Yeah. He's, um, really good." He closed the door behind him, stepping fully into the room.

"Ro. Don't." Justin was back in the living room.

Don't what? Scold him in front of Shane? Yell at him? Question his motives? Yell at Shane for giving him a job.

"Justin. You're 18 now. You can do whatever you want. I just think there're other things you can do with your time. And Shane," Rowan turned back to him, piercing him with a death stare. "You put him in a situation where he gets hurt or gets in trouble, you will have to deal with me. Got that?"

Shane looked up at Justin and then glanced back to Rowan, smiling, "Easy Mama Bear. Justin's really good at this stuff and can handle himself better than most out there. But I get your message loud and clear."

Justin laughed as he walked away, repeating Mama Bear over and over again like that was the biggest joke in the world.

Rowan's eyes softened and she relaxed. "Hi."

"Hi."

"I guess I owe you an apology, too. I left this morning a little, um, abruptly."

"That's okay. I told you, it doesn't matter, this is happening. I can wait out your panic attacks." Shane stepped forward.

"Panic attacks?" *God, was she that obvious?*

Shane smiled at her and closed the gap between them. "Yeah, babe. I told you, I can see when your brain is working overdrive. You're a mystery most of the time, but that I can see. I think it's kinda cute, actually."

"Kinda cute?" Rowan said on a laugh. "That's a little strange, even for you."

He reached up and wrapped his large hand around the base of her neck, his thumb caressing her chin.

"Even for me, huh? Like I'm deranged or something?" He smiled at her, his face dipping down close to hers, his lips brushing lightly on hers.

"Excuse me." Justin's voice broke through the room.

Shane and Rowan broke apart and looked up at Justin.

"So, um, Ro. I'm going to shower and go out. Are you going to be here or at Shane's tonight?" Justin asked, looking anywhere but at Rowan.

Rowan froze. Justin was dating someone! And he wanted the apartment again. Good God!

"Justin, do we need to have a chat?" Rowan raised her eyebrow at him questioningly.

A laugh forced its way out of his mouth and he just looked at her. "Yeah Ro, you're a few years too late on that one. Are you going to be here or not?"

Rowan sucked in her breath. Jesus.

"She'll be at my place." Shane stepped in and saved

them both from the most awkward conversation two people could have.

"Great. Thanks." Justin looked at Shane and turned around.

"Justin!" Rowan called out to him, "We'll revisit this later."

"Great. Can't wait," Justin muttered, sounding exactly like the teenager he was.

•   •   •

"Why don't you change into something nice and I'll take you out?" Shane said after Justin disappeared into the back.

"Out out?" Rowan asked.

He smiled at her. God, she was beautiful. In her confusion her eyes were round saucers filled with glowing brown orbs.

"Yes. Out out. As in nice restaurant. As in date with my girlfriend," Shane challenged. He knew he was pushing her, but he wanted her to know how serious he was.

"Oh," she said, then smiled. "Okay. I'll come down to your place when I'm ready."

He kissed her and turned to leave. "Don't take too long, or else I'll come back and drag you out of here," he said as he walked out the door.

Nearly skipping down the stairs because she didn't balk at the girlfriend reference, his heart was soaring as he opened his apartment. He'd take a quick shower and clean up the place a bit. He knew just where to take her, even had the connections to get a table, so he had time to prep for the after dinner part of the evening.

Twenty minutes later he was showered, dressed in

slacks and a nice shirt, no tie—he thought that would be a little over the top. It was still too hot for his leather jacket, but cool enough that long sleeves would be comfortable.

Forty minutes later his apartment was clean, a bottle of wine was in the fridge, and his bed had fresh sheets on it. He had candles set up for later, putting the final dishes away and wiping down his bathroom counters.

Fifty minutes later he was pacing. Fifty minutes. How long does it take to get ready? He checked his watch for the millionth time. He would wait one hour then go back up there and get her. She was probably in another panic attack because of his girlfriend comment. He shouldn't have said that. *Too early. Way to blow it, Adams.*

Sixty minutes later and he'd had enough. Grabbing his keys and storming to the door, he flung it open, blood pumping, ready for a fight, and nearly slammed right into her. He jerked himself back, hoping like hell he didn't run into her.

"Hi," she said shyly.

Taking her in, he felt his blood race again, although this time not from fear or anger, but from desire. She was stunning. She wore a purple dress that hugged her body like a dancer and fell loose around her legs, accentuating her sinfully perfect curves. My god, he might die of a heart attack; he'd never seen such magnificent beauty in all his life. His breath simply stopped.

"Um. Are you okay?" she asked again after a few seconds.

Shane let out the breath he was holding. "Yeah," he croaked out, "Yeah. I'm perfect."

If it was possible, her eyes glowed even brighter at

his response. She shook her hair out of her eyes and tilted her head, watching him. "You ready?"

"Yep," he said again on a breath, this time regaining some ability to speak. "Let's go." Offering her his arm after he shut the door, he shook his head a little trying to clear it.

Smiling, she slipped her arm in his. Shane couldn't even feel the ground; he was floating so high right now. He had, without a doubt, the most beautiful woman alive on his arm. And, it would appear as if she had agreed to be his girlfriend. His chest was filling with something he couldn't explain and that was okay with him; he was happy.

And proud: This was better than solving the toughest case out there, better than winning a million dollars, better than anything in the world. He couldn't stop the grin spreading across his face.

He opened her car door for her and watched her settle into the seat. Closing it, he practically skipped over to the driver's side. Jesus, he needed to get a little control over himself.

They drove in almost silence to the restaurant. Shane kept stealing glances at her, afraid that if he waited too long to look at her she would disappear. Every once in awhile he would catch her eye watching him, too. He hoped that was a good thing.

"Can I ask you something?" he broke the silence.

"Maybe?" she answered, coyly.

"What are you thinking right now?" Grabbing her hand when he spoke, he just needed to touch her. To remind himself that this was real.

"I'm thinking that you look really happy. And handsome." She turned her head away from him when she spoke.

"Hey." He gently grabbed her chin and brought her

head back around to him. "Don't be shy, Rowan. You can tell me anything. Nothing you say to me should make you embarrassed."

"I was thinking that you look really good tonight. Hot, even." She looked him right in the eye, heat making her eyes glow even in the dark car.

Shane felt his cock move in his pants. This woman was going to bring him to his knees. She had no idea, but she already owned him.

"Thanks," he said, forcing his eyes back on the road.

His heart was racing again. *Easy, Adams.* Tonight wasn't about a quick roll in the hay. This was about showing Rowan how serious he was about her. This woman had flipped his world upside down. Never had he been this serious about a woman. He'd had plenty of girlfriends, one-night stands, even a few friends with benefits in his time, but never had they elicited such a reaction from him.

His heart was both elated and scared. Rowan made him want to shout from the rooftops that she was his and stash her away, all at the same time. He felt completely confident they were meant for each other, but he was so scared she would run from him and disappear, he could barely breathe. If he let the feelings take over he might curl up in a ball and never move, so he was plowing through this the only way he knew how: One moment at a time.

Glancing over at Rowan, he caught her eye and they both smiled at each other. Truth be told, she looked exactly like he felt. Oh please, let that be true! He hoped she was feeling just as wild about this whole thing as he was.

Pulling into the Sheraton Teahouse, he stopped in front of the valet.

"Wait, where are we?" She suddenly had that panicked look in her eyes again.

"This is the nicest place in town. Is this okay?" he turned to her, having pulled his keys out of the ignition.

Before she could answer, both doors opened and a hand was offered to her. He turned and got out the car, handing the keys to valet.

"Mr. Adams, nice to see you again," the valet said, handing him his ticket.

"Hey, Frank. How's it going? Still seeing Becky?" Shane asked him.

Frank was a good guy, a little young, but he freelanced with him whenever he needed extra money.

"You know it. I may be dumb, but I'm not stupid." Frank wiggled his eyes at him and slipped into the Kia.

Shane walked over to where Rowan was standing, looking like a deer in headlights.

"Rowan. Seriously. Are you okay?" he asked as they walked into the restaurant.

She shook her head slightly, but looked pale and tense. Her shoulders were up around her ears, her eyes looked vacant.

"Rowan." He stopped her and spun her around to meet his eyes. "It's okay. We don't have to come here."

"No, it's fine. I just didn't know where we were going. I'm feeling, um, a little under dressed. That's all." She paused and smiled a tight smile at him.

"Mr. Adams, how nice to see you again," the maître d' said, greeting them both.

"Do you know everyone here?" she asked under her breath, glaring at him.

She sounded really mad. Maybe that's just her feeling insecure, but man, she sounded pissed that he knew the people that worked here. Women! Fuck if he knew what the hell just happened.

He stepped up to the maître d' and smiled, holding Rowan's hand tight, dragging her along with him.

"Hello, Mr. Edwards. How are you this evening? We would love the most romantic table you have," Shane said, not letting Rowan get more than an arm's length away from him. He was not going to let her run because she felt under dressed. She was the most beautiful woman here, by far.

He heard her intake of breath on his request. Pulling her closer, he wrapped his arm around her, his hand settling on her low back. He guided her as they followed Mr. Edwards to their table. As they arrived, he held out her chair and she sat with all the grace of a queen, placing her napkin on her lap.

Shane watched as her features changed from upset to resigned to masked. The more masked she became, the more graceful she seemed. All the hard edges melted away and she sat looking poised and ready. Whatever was going on in her head, she was not relaxed or enjoying herself. She was putting on a damn good front, but it wasn't fooling him.

He settled into his chair and waited for the Mr. Edwards to leave. Finally, he turned to her and watched as she scanned the room with cold eyes. She was back to her usual habits, he noted.

"You have nothing to be wary about, Rowan. You are the most well dressed, elegant, beautiful woman here," he told her quietly.

Rowan gave him a hard stare and opened her mouth. But then she closed it again and looked away. When her eyes returned to him they were softer, her features less masked and her shoulders had fallen a few inches from her ears.

"This is lovely, Shane. I just didn't expect to come here. That's all. I was taken by surprise. I'm not really a surprise kind of person," she said on an exhale.

Shane laughed. "Right. So no surprise birthday parties, then. When is your birthday?"

"8-3-83." Rowan answered in rhyme.

"Oh, so you just had one, then. Just last month. Now I have to wait a whole year to celebrate with you." He paused, his eyes shining into hers.

She laughed. "Well, it's never been much of a celebration. But yeah. Just turned 31. God, that sounds so old."

"Easy. You're talking to a 32 year old. From where I'm sitting, 31 looks mighty fine to me," he said, hoping she'd get his double entendre.

Her eyes flashed for a second and then she laughed again, relaxing back to the Rowan he was used to. No more extra grace, no masks, just two people having a nice dinner.

She didn't seem to have an opinion on the food or the wine, so Shane ordered a variety of small plates for them to share, liking the idea of the two of them eating off the same plates. Of course, now that Rowan was back to her old self, he was much more relaxed and looking forward to the rest of the evening.

• • •

The wine was amazing and the food left her dizzy, it was so good. She was well fed and her head was swimming with all the appreciative looks from Shane. He was so attentive and kind. Every look he gave her, every question he asked her, every touch of his hand, opened her heart a little more. Before the end of the evening she felt like she was truly in a bubble. There was nothing wrong in this place. No need to run, no need to worry, no need to scan the room for people or exits. Jolly never existed here and never would. This was her safe place. Her special cocoon with Shane.

When they first arrived she thought she was going to throw up. It was too late to change meeting places with Lina. She would just have to risk it and hope that nobody remembered her. Of all places Shane could have taken her, what were the odds that they ended up here? And he knew everyone! She thought she was going to die of fear those first few moments.

But then Shane was so kind and thought she was just nervous about being in a really nice place. It never occurred to him that anything else was at play here. That was one of the things she loved about him. He was just so sweet and open. Yes, he was a PI, so he had to be suspicious by nature, but with Rowan he never suspected anything. She could completely relax with him. He would never hurt her. She knew that now.

She watched as Shane paid the bill, again making her feel like a real, treasured princess. At they stood, he once again placed his hand on her lower back. She felt his heat radiate across her body, relishing the feeling. She just felt so, so, what was the word. Dare she think, loved?

Her breath lodged in her throat with the thought. He paused and looked at her quizzically. She shook her head, clearing her brain of those thoughts, and smiled up at him as he led her back out of the restaurant to the valet.

"Mr. Adams." The same valet spoke to him when they stepped outside. "Your car will be right out."

Shane nodded then nuzzled his head into hers. She couldn't help but lean into his touch. She loved the feeling of him surrounding her. Her skin reacted to his touch like nothing she had ever felt before. It was as if her cells were speaking to his and she was just the conduit between them. She liked being the conduit.

Shane growled low and deep into her ear, causing her nerves to fire. She looked up at him through her lashes and smiled a knowing smile.

"Home, then?" she asked, coyly.

"Oh yeah, home right now. You need to be in my bed, naked," he all but growled at her.

Her skin pebbled with the sound of his voice. She could feel her nipples harden and moisture slick her panties. Letting out a breath, she shook her head.

Just then, the car drove up and Shane opened her door for her. Slipping in, she watched him as he made his way across the car, handing Frank a tip.

"Call me anytime," he said to Frank as he opened the door.

When they pulled out of the parking lot, Rowan asked him, "So, you and — Frank, was it? How do you know each other?"

"Frankie freelances with me every once in a while. He's pretty good, too, but he only does it when he needs some extra cash," Shane explained while holding her hand.

"I didn't know you could just slip in and out of PI work?" she said, genuinely interested.

"Well, only if you know a PI. Rob and Cody are my partners, but sometimes you just need someone to sit in the car with you to stay awake. Frank tells a mean joke and never drinks coffee, so he is an ideal stakeout partner." Shane laughed at whatever joke he was remembering.

It was nice to see Shane so relaxed and happy about his work. With a small regret, Rowan realized that she had never asked him about his work. She was just too afraid of it all. Tonight she wasn't afraid. Tonight she was just his girlfriend. Her heart lifted with that thought; she was Shane's girlfriend.

"So, that's what you do? Sit in cars all night?"

"Yeah, that's part of it. We also find missing people and track down evidence for lawyers. Rob has had some intense missing persons cases where we've found several young women in bad shape. I think they were headed into forced prostitution."

Rowan was shocked; she sort of remembered him mentioning something like that a long time ago, but she never really registered what he had been telling her. These guys were rescuing girls from forced prostitution? She had no idea that PIs did that kind of thing. She had never really thought about it before. She just knew that PIs could be hired to find people. People that most likely didn't want to be found.

Shane kept his hand on her body the whole way back, only taking it off her leg to shift gears and then he would wrap his large hand around her thigh again. She liked the feeling of it. She could feel his warmth sinking into her, and the loss of it when he needed his hand to drive.

Rowan didn't know what was happening here, but she was so tired of fighting it. Letting her head fall back against the seat and closing her eyes, she didn't want to be on the run anymore, she didn't want to worry about tomorrow, she wanted to let go of all of it. Couldn't she do that—just let go of it all and really feel what was happening to her? The closer they got to the apartments, the more relaxed she became. She was going to be Shane's girlfriend. She had never been anyone's girlfriend before. Loving the sound of it, she giggled a little.

"Hey now. Am I losing you?" Shane asked, squeezing her thigh.

Rowan smiled a sultry smile at him and shook her head. "Quite the contrary, Shane. You have me. I feel like I'm finally showing up to the party."

Pulling the car into the lot, he looked over at her, his eyes flashing when they connected with hers.

"Good," he said, gruffly, "About time, too."

Jumping out, he came around to her side while she opened her door and reached in to help her out. Once again, he placed his hand right at the base of her spine, sending shivers up and down her body. She couldn't help the smile that crept across her face.

Once through the door, Shane pounced on her. Twisting her hands into his short hair brought a thrill all its own, so silky and short, but what really sent her into orbit was the way his body quivered under her touch. His hands wrapped around her head, holding her close. His mouth devoured her, while his marauding tongue searched the inside of hers.

Rowan opened for him and moaned when she felt his hot tongue slide inside her mouth. His hands pressed her yet closer to him, smoothing down her body and pressing her pelvis into his hard length.

"Naked. Now," he demanded.

She didn't hesitate, already ripping off her dress and sliding her panties down her legs. Shane clawed at the clasp of her bra and launched it off of her. He stepped back, admiring her naked body.

"Goddamn, Rowan. Nothing better. Nothing goddamn better than you naked." He spoke as if she wasn't even in the room.

"Um. You naked would be a good start," she told him, hoping to snap him out of his reverie.

Shane didn't have to be told twice. He slipped his

shoes off while unbuckling his pants. While he slipped his pants down, he tossed his shirt aside, leaving him in his underwear.

She swallowed hard. Nothing would have prepared her for seeing him naked like that. Yeah, she had seen him before, but each and every time took her breath away. His erection was straining against the cotton, making her hands itch to hold him.

"Jesus. You are by far the sexist man I have ever laid eyes on. I can't believe I'm here with you," she breathed out, trying to calm her blood.

"Believe me, baby. I feel the same way about you," he told her as he crossed the room, closing the gap between them.

This time he wrapped his large hand around the base of her neck and the other around her waist. Rowan shivered while her blood flashed hot. Her hands flew down to unleash him. She needed him raw, just like she was. He needed to be completely bare and at her mercy.

She dropped to her knees, wrapping her hand around his cock. God, it was so beautiful! And big. Jesus. Her hand looked tiny next to him. There was no way she was going to get the entire thing in her mouth; instead she licked from root to tip, listening to Shane moan.

When she felt bolder, she opened her mouth as wide as she could and took him in. She could get about half inside her mouth, but she felt her teeth scrape across the sides of his length. She knew that wasn't good, so she tried again. Soon she was using her lips to cover her teeth and found a nice rhythm with her mouth and hands.

Whatever she was doing seemed to be working for Shane. He hadn't spoken a word since she pulled him into her mouth. His hands were on either side of her head and his hips were moving slowly. When she stole a glance at his face, she saw that his eyes were closed and he had the most amazing look of ecstasy on his face. Rowan had never seen a man look like that before. He held nothing back.

When she felt his balls tighten, she knew he was close. He moaned again and thrust harder into her. A thrill shot through her system at the thought of him coming in her mouth. She opened wider, trying to take more of him in. He growled.

"Rowan. I'm going to come. If you don't want me to, you gotta stop, baby. I can't stop it," He spat out, sounding as if the words were painful.

She took more of him in, this time almost all of him, and slowly drew him out. Over and over again, slow and steady, soft and hard.

"Oh God. Yes. Fuucckk!" Shane roared as the first hot liquid of his release spilled out of him. She liked the taste and sucked harder. More leaked out and she swallowed all of it. He was breathing heavy, his knees were collapsing. She finally let him go and stood up, guiding him to the couch.

He sat, pulling her on top of him, burying his head in her hair. She felt so safe wrapped in his arms, surrounded by his body. His hands roamed her slowly while his breathing steadied. With each pass he got closer and closer to the very core of her. She was still wet, still fired up, her nerves on fire, and she shivered uncontrollably with his touch.

He held her close and teased her with his magic hands. Soon she couldn't take it anymore and lay her head on his chest, her body still draped across his, open and exposed to him.

"Hmm. I like this," he said under his breath.

His hands roamed over her breasts and down her sides, running up and down her flat stomach. Finally, his fingers found her curls and brushed down her folds. She felt his finger dip inside and come out wet, causing Shane to growl.

"Please," she begged, her single plea as his hands drifted away from her again. He chuckled and came back to her. His hands brushed against her once again and a fire rose from between her legs to the top of her head while a moan, low and deep, ripped out of her.

His fingers found her entrance and his thumb found her clit. She convulsed as two fingers slide inside of her. When his thumb scraped across her clit her hips flew off of him, and she cried out.

He held her down and did it again. And again. With every swipe, an electric force built inside of her. His fingers thrust in and out of her, harder and harder, coating her inner thighs with her wetness. With every pass of his thumb it felt as if she was being touched with a live wire. The pleasure was so intense, she could feel the blood rushing in her ears. Her toes curled and she knew she was close now.

"Shane," she said or moaned, she couldn't tell which, "Oh God." The pleasure took over, the electricity rose from her toes and spread deliciously throughout her entire body.

"Yeeessss!" she cried.

Sweat misted her body and her hips moved on their own, thrusting into his hands. The blood in her ears sounded like a freight train as her orgasm roared through her body, finally leaving her slack and panting, still spread out on top of Shane.

• • •

A Sex Goddess, that's what she was — Aphrodite was on top of him, panting and moaning. He couldn't believe it. He was the luckiest guy on the planet! And, he was rock hard again. Shane ran his hands up and down her lean legs, feeling her soft skin and toned muscle underneath his fingertips.

When he thought she could move, he helped her sit up and led her to the bedroom. He needed to be inside of her, that was his heaven. Never had anything felt so all consuming before. He needed it more than an addict needed his next fix.

Rowan still looked a little blown away, so he paused in the bedroom and wrapped his arms around her small, perfect body. Inhaling her scent filled him with more hope and optimism than a thousand Christmas mornings. This woman held the key to life and he knew that his would never be the same.

"Rowan," he whispered into her ear, "Let me make love to you tonight. Please," he begged her.

She went slack on him and buried her head in his chest. Slowly, she nodded, and he picked her up and carried her to the bed. Gently placing her on the sheet, his eyes roamed her body as she lay there. When their eyes collided, he was taken aback with the amount of heat and emotion he saw reflected back at him. It was clear she wanted him as much as he wanted her.

Without waiting any longer, Shane leaned down on top of her, using his knee to open her legs. He took one hand and slipped on the condom and then found the place he needed most. With one swift push, he was inside heaven.

"Oh God!" slipped out before he could stop himself. There was just nothing better than right now, right here.

Slowly at first, he started to move, finding a nice, solid

rhythm. Watching her eyes, so big and trusting, it felt as if he could see straight to her soul. She was opening up to him, giving him a guarded piece of herself. His insides burned and his cock jumped inside of her with the thought. Her eyes widened in surprise and she smiled.

That was it. Shane was a goner. He knew he couldn't take much more. She was just too damn perfect. He dropped his head and closed his eyes, letting his hips take over. He could hear Rowan's heavy breathing and moaning.

"I'm not going to last, baby. It's just too damn good with you," he groaned.

Rowan sat up slightly, causing his angle to change, allowing him to go deeper. She propped herself on her elbows and dropped her head back. Goddamn Aphro-fucking-dite.

"Right there," she said as she lifted her hips slightly when he slammed into her, "Oh God, right there."

He watched her as her orgasm built, desperately trying to hold off his own, waiting for her.

"Harder," she moaned.

"Fuck!" Shane gave up holding back and slammed her hard, over and over again. He felt the tingles rise along his spine and his balls tighten. There was nothing he could do to stop his own orgasm now; he just prayed she got there fast enough.

"Yes," she yelled out, "That's it."

He couldn't hear anything else as the roar in his ears took over and he emptied inside of her.

After a few minutes, maybe an hour, he slid out of her and got up to take care of the condom. When he came back to bed, Rowan lay there sound asleep, her beauty spilling onto the sheets. Walking back into the living room, he got some water and looked for their clothes, chuckling a little when he could only find her underwear. Leaving hers next to her side of the bed, he went back to his side, turning off all the lights and slipping underneath the covers to spoon the vixen beauty that now shared his bed.

CHAPTER THIRTEEN

The phone rang out in the darkened room. Shane groaned and tried to ignore it, but it wouldn't stop. He felt Rowan sit up.

"Shane, answer the phone so it'll shut up already," she said, groping around.

"Shit," he cursed and sat up, grabbing the damn device. "This had better be good."

"Rob needs you. I'm outside your door. Get your ass up and come outside," Justin's voice jolted Shane out of his slumber.

"Yeah. You bet. Give me two minutes," he said, much more alert than a second before.

"Is this going to be a regular thing with you? 'Cause it sorta sucks," she said with a sleepy smile on her face.

He leaned over and kissed her. "Naw. Just while Rob is working this case, shit comes up."

He leapt out of bed and grabbed a pair of jeans and a shirt. Dressing quickly, he checked his gun, then picked up his phone and keys. Leaning over one more time to kiss Rowan before heading out the door, he found she was already asleep, so he kissed her lightly on the lips and walked out.

Justin was waiting for him just outside. Without

speaking, they walked toward the parking lot, Justin taking the lead heading to his truck. Shane nodded as he got in the passenger seat while Justin started the engine.

"What's going down?"

"Same shit as always. Rob's got some room in a house he wants to see what's inside, and there are three guys in the house at all times," Justin answered.

"Great. You dragged my ass out of bed for another fucking pot farm." Shane laughed, shaking his head.

• • •

Rowan woke with a start, her hair on the back of her neck standing up. Someone was in the apartment and the way her body was reacting, it wasn't Shane. Without moving, she listened to the silence. As soon as she thought it was just a dream she heard the distant sound of a door slowly clicking shut.

Definitely not Shane. Footsteps sounded off the walls, nothing that would have woken her up, but now that she was awake and listening, she could hear their uneven fall. She got up and grabbed her underwear while looking for the rest. Damn it, she'd undressed in the living room.

Looking around the room, Rowan searched for anything that could help her. Shane took his phone and she didn't have one. There was one in the office; she needed to make it to the office. Without thinking more about what she was wearing, she slipped out of the bedroom to make her way down the hall.

The intruder was not nearly as quiet as Rowan was. He was creeping around the kitchen. She could make out his outline. He, too, seemed to be searching for something, opening cabinets and rummaging through them. Every once in awhile he would pause and wipe his forehead as if he was sweating a lot.

Excellent. Rowan had some crazy SOB, high on something, looking for chocolate in the goddamn kitchen. As she turned to head into the office, her eye caught the distant flash of metal in the back of his pants. *Oh, it gets even better. The guy is carrying.*

Slipping into the office, she closed the door. She waited a few seconds to see if he noticed the click of the latch bolt, but she couldn't hear him moving around and figured he was still in the kitchen looking for snacks. Making her way to the phone, she picked it up and dialed 911.

"State your emergency, please," the dispatcher answered in her bored, I-do-this-all-day-long voice. She guessed it was supposed to be soothing, but it was just irritating.

Rowan spoke softly but clearly, stating her address and apartment number. Whenever the dispatcher tried to interrupt her, she talked over her. She whispered calmly into the phone, telling her that there was an intruder in her apartment going through her kitchen and that he was armed. And then, without waiting for the operator to ask her more questions, she hung up.

Looking around the room for help, she noticed a pile of toys left over from when the kids were here. Walking over to assess what treasures they had left behind, she found a toy gun. Picking it up, she stared at it. It was all black and looked just like the real thing, except the bright orange tip at the end. That tip glinted off the light, calling out to anyone within 50 feet that this was a toy. Damn.

Looking around again for something better, her head started spinning. She could do this. She did it a hundred times before. She had the element of surprise;

she could just come out of this room and disarm him. She knew how. But—she shuddered at the thought. She did not want to go back to that headspace. Did not want to fall back on her training. She hated the training.

A bump from the other room brought her back to the present moment. There was an armed man in this apartment and she needed get her shit together, right now. Listening, she could hear him walking down the hall, he was not quiet, not even in the least, making her wonder if he had checked the bedroom and decided he was alone.

He was headed this way, that she was sure of. She could hear his footsteps in the hall right outside. *Shit shit shit.* Rowan looked at the toy gun in her hand and heard the man getting closer. She stopped thinking and just reacted. Putting the plastic orange ring in her mouth, she bit down hard. When she felt it crack, she bit down again, feeling the bits of sharp plastic in her mouth.

Spitting into her hand, she looked at the gun. It wasn't perfect, but it was better than a neon orange ring blowing her cover. Putting her ear to the door, she waited. Listening to the sounds in the hall, her body tensed up. All her muscles were getting ready for a fight, adrenaline pumping in her bloodstream like a fire hose, and she was having a hard time staying calm. Waiting. This was the part that always tripped her up in training. As soon as she had a plan and felt that surge into her blood, she wanted to go. To get it over with.

This time though, she waited. She needed to surprise him at the perfect moment. She went through her training, reviewed her options, and felt the moment she was ready. She could have been in the

Arena, or even the Big House, it didn't matter now, she was ready. The door handle twitched. He was right outside this door, about to come in. She pressed her body to the doorframe and watched the handle. Slowly, it moved and the door opened a hair's breadth. Swinging the door open, she stepped in front him, gun to his forehead.

"Holy Shit!" the guy squeaked, jerking back his head.

"Hi, asshole. You're in the wrong house," Rowan barked at him.

"Jesus, are you naked?" he asked, his eyes roaming across her chest.

"Turn around, motherfucker. Or I'll kill you right now." Once again, she barked out her commands in the deepest voice she had.

His eyes widened in surprise, but he didn't move.

She stared him down and moved her hands, as if she was balancing the gun and aiming. Real guns were heavy and weighted just so with a full clip. This one was plastic and weighed about three ounces. She hoped she pulled it off.

The guy slowly turned around, bringing his hands up.

She slipped the gun out of his pants.

"What the fuck you need this for, asshole? You steal this from your daddy?" She picked it up and looked at it. Glock 17, just like her old one. With a full clip inside, if she wasn't mistaken. One in the chamber.

"You always walk around other people's homes with a fully loaded gun? What a fucking idiot. Walk." Rowan marched him back to the front room. She still held the fake gun at him, but kept ahold of his, just in case.

When they got to the front room, she stopped him

and told him to open the curtain. She knew, or at least hoped, that the cops were coming, and she wanted them to know exactly what apartment they were needed in. He complied.

"Now lie down," she barked.

"No fucking way, lady. I'm walking outta here," he said as he started to turn toward her.

Reacting quickly, she hit him on the head with his loaded gun. He went down like a solid mass, hitting the floor with a loud thump. With one hand she released the clip and let it fall just to her left. She still had one in the chamber; that was all she really needed anyway. She dropped the toy gun and kicked out his hands and feet, keeping the gun aimed at his head. She stood just outside his strike zone. He was out, but he might wake up. She knew that trick and this time she would be ready.

Rowan stood over the man. Waiting. Remembering.

• • •

The sirens were right behind them when Justin pulled into traffic. They watched as six police cars and an ambulance raced past Justin's truck. Shane was tired, the night took a lot out of him, and he needed to sleep. Justin looked tired, too.

They made their way back to the apartment, but as they got close, all they could see were red and blue flashing lights. Something big was going down inside their complex. Shane's first thought was of Rowan, but then he laughed it off, until he glanced over at Justin and saw that he, too, looked tense.

"Wonder what's going on?" Justin asked him as they tried to pull in.

A police officer stopped them just as they got to the driveway.

"Sorry guys. This is off limits. We got a police action going on in one of the apartments."

Just then, a voice boomed through a bullhorn, "Ma'am, put the gun down and get on the floor."

Justin didn't hesitate; he was out the door and sprinting to the apartment. Shane followed just a few steps behind him. He didn't know why Justin was running, but if he was running, so was Shane.

When Shane looked up at his apartment, his heart stopped. There was Rowan, naked, holding a gun on someone. Jesus. As he crept closer, the chaos around him seemed to fade away and all he could focus on was Rowan. She was in a wide stance, just a few feet from some guy sprawled out on the floor. She was aiming the gun at his head. She wasn't responding to the police, just stared at the guy on the floor, waiting for something.

"Fuck." Justin's curse tore through his thoughts and he turned to see the swat team gearing up.

"Wait!" Shane called out to one of the guys. "That's my apartment and my girlfriend; she can be there. The guy on the floor is an intruder," he shouted to anyone who would listen.

Justin followed him. When they got close to the window, Justin shouted, "RO. RO." But an officer blocked him from going further.

"Who are you and what are you doing here?" He scowled down at him.

"I'm Justin. I live with her. Fuck. She needs me right now." Justin sounded frantic.

"And you are?" The officer turned to Shane.

"I'm her boyfriend and that's my apartment," Shane

told him, sounding even more frustrated than before. "Where's Sargent Brooks?"

"Well, if you can get her to put the gun down we can go in and assess the situation."

Justin bolted and ran up to the window, banging on it. Rowan turned her head and saw him.

"Rowan. Put the gun down. Drill is over. Disarm and protect," Justin shouted into the glass.

Shane had no idea what he was talking about, but something snapped in Rowan's eyes. She nodded and slid the hammer back, dislodging the chamber bullet and dropping the gun. The police charged in and took her down. Shane watched, enraged as they swarmed her small, naked body and handcuffed her.

Justin paced outside, looking just as freaked out as he felt. After a few minutes they brought her out. God damn it, she still didn't have a shirt on. What was wrong with these guys, he didn't recognize any of them. He took off his and walked up to her, but was stopped by a large officer walking in front of them.

"Jesus. Put a goddamn shirt on her," Shane growled at him, thrusting his shirt into the officer's hands.

He watched as the officer turned around and put the shirt over her head, finally covering her. Her hands were still behind her back, but at least she was wearing something.

Justin appeared out of nowhere and stepped right in front of her.

"You did great, Ro. Please don't. Just don't, you did great," He told her, his voice cracking. Her eyes looked up at him, just slightly less vacant now that he was there.

"I'm sorry, but family only. We need to take her statement now," The officer leading her barked at him.

"In handcuffs?" Shane exploded at him. "You need to take her statement in handcuffs?"

The officer paused and then nodded to the other one standing beside her. He reached down and unlocked them. Rowan moved her arms through the holes in the shirt and looked at Shane. He moved forward but was once again stopped by the monster in uniform.

"You can wait, Mister. Family only," he barked at him again.

God, what an asshole.

"I'm her son," Justin spoke up.

Shane's head jerked up, looking at him. *What?*

"Is that true, Miss?" the monster asked Rowan.

"Yes sir," Rowan barely spoke, "Yes, Justin is my son. I'd like him to come."

A NOTE FROM THE AUTHOR

Thank you for reading the first part of Escape. Rowan and Shane's story unfolds in a three part romantic suspense series. The Series continues with Escaping With Eve (Justin's Story) and Rob and Cody's stories. If you enjoyed Part One, please think about leaving a review. To be notified as soon as the next books in this series are released, join my mailing list www.SydneyHolmes.com/contact-sydney

My first big thank you is to you—the readers! I'm thrilled you read my book. I loved writing it and hope you enjoyed it as much as I did.

Once again, Valerie from Loud Lit Chicks, swooped in and saved the day! Thanks Valerie, your work remains invaluable.

Karen not only designed the cover, but she has been my greatest champion from the very beginning. Thanks Karen, what would I do without you?

Of course, I wouldn't be here today without my husband. Somehow I married the most amazing man on the planet. Words cannot express my love for you and all you do. Thank you from the recesses of my heart.

And last but most definitely not least, I would like to thank my amazing beta readers! Without you, life just wouldn't be the same.

MEET SYDNEY

Sydney Holmes, a *USA Today* best-selling author, writes alluring mysteries to spice up your night! Writing mysteries is a dream come true. Sydney writes thrilling mysteries and provocative romance because she loves lascivious men and strong, confident, women. She believes there are few things as exciting as reading a great book about two people searching for each other, and finding themselves. Add in a murder, kidnapping or a decades old mystery and it just doesn't get any better.

Sydney is happily married with two children. She graduated from The George Washington University with a Bachelor's degree in Political Science and holds a Master's degree in Education. She lives near the ocean in California and travels as often as she can.

To learn more about Sydney, please visit her website at www.SydneyHolmes.com. Or, check her out on Facebook www.FaceBook.com/SydneyHolmesAuthor And, follow her on Twitter @SydHolmesAuthor

For periodic updates, news, events, book releases, and sneak peeks please join Sydney's mailing list at www.SydneyHolmes.com/contact-sydney.

Excerpt from

ESCAPE
Part 2

CHAPTER ONE

Rain! The first sign that this God awful summer was finally coming to an end. He could almost hear the concrete sizzling as the rainwater cooled it. Stepping to the window, Shane watched as the water splashed into the pool, rain puddling on the sidewalk. He knew exactly how that water felt; slow, hot and going nowhere.

His eyes darted upstairs to Rowan's door. It looked like all the other doors in this complex, but unlike those other doors, this one invoked emotions he was not so comfortable with. He knew what was behind that door, and he irrationally blamed it for keeping her from him. It had been weeks since he had seen her. Weeks since that horrible night he found out that Justin was her son. Her son!

At first, he was giving her space to deal with the break in. Then he was giving her space to let her get comfortable with the fact that he knew her long protected secret. And now he was just giving her space.

Twice he had walked up there and knocked. Once there was no answer, but he knew she was in there. The other time, Justin answered the door and sent him away with an apologetic grimace. Now, he just stood in his apartment and watched her door—back to the same creepy stalker tactics from a while ago.

Justin was her son. At first he'd wondered what kind of mother hides that, but then he did the math. He couldn't believe it at first, even worked it out on paper. The math didn't make sense, but everything else clicked into place. Hindsight is, in fact, 20/20. It was so obvious now that he knew. Their maddening personality traits, their eyes: although Rowan's were brown and Justin's were green, they shared that bright light within, making their eyes appear as if they were glowing. Their interactions were so mother/son. So much so that Shane had started questioning his PI skills.

Obvious yes, but the age difference was frightening. Rowan had to have been twelve or thirteen when she had him. Who has a kid at twelve? How does that even happen? His blood started to boil every time he thought of twelve year old Rowan in that situation. What man would take such innocence?

And when he wasn't doing math and wondering what fucker out there needed to die a painful death for knocking up a twelve year old, he would flash back to the night of the break in. Rowan standing over the perp, gun drawn and ready. In her underwear, no less. She was what, 5 feet 4 inches and 110 pounds, maybe? She took down a crazed drug addict twice her size practically naked, with a toy gun! He couldn't even pull that off.

The rain picked up, battering the window and drowning out his thoughts. He watched it for a while longer before turning back to his work. He wanted to see Rowan, but he needed to finish his case reports first. Rowan knew he was waiting for her, and when she was ready she would come out of her cave and find him. He was sure of it. He just wasn't so sure how much longer he was going to be patient.

~

Shane pulled into the parking lot of his apartment in a foul mood. Why do some clients have to be such assholes? It wasn't his fault that their spouse was cheating, or their business partner was skimming money, or their boss was stealing their ideas. He was just the messenger. If they really didn't want to know, why the hell did they hire him in the first place?

That's what this week had become, a week of cheaters, skimmers, and thieves. And all he really wanted to do was find a beer and forget about it all. This was not what he signed up for when he went into this business.

Shane parked and got out of his car, slamming the door harder than he meant to. Just great, now he was going to break the damn car, too. Storming into his apartment, he threw down his keys, walking straight to the fridge. Thank Fuck he remembered to buy beer yesterday. Finally, something he did right.

Cool, bittersweet liquid poured down his throat. Ah! Feeling his shoulders drop and his jaw unclench, he felt better instantly; that was just what he needed. What a fucking day. That Evans woman can be such a pain in the ass! All he could tell her was that her boss was, in fact, stealing her ideas and presenting them as her own. What he couldn't answer for her was why. If he had to hazard a guess, it was because they were all good ideas. Did they really need to discuss it for two hours?

Rolling his neck from side to side while pacing around his apartment, he felt himself get more and more wound up. Usually his place was welcoming and relaxing, but tonight it felt too small, compounding his agitation. Walking over to the window, he took another sip of beer.

Justin's truck was not in the lot. Come to think of it, Shane hadn't seen Rowan's car, either. That was different. He glanced up at her door again and almost choked on his beer. There was Rowan at the top of stairs. God, he almost forgot how beautiful she was.

He watched her as she pulled out her key and unlocked the door. Her movements were graceful and calculated, making him think that something was wrong. Scanning the area he found nothing amiss and glanced back up the stairs just in time to see her slip inside and shut the door. He stood, his heart hammering in his chest, fighting the urge to storm up there and demand to talk to her.

Instead, he drank his beer and tried to get his body under control. Even if he was going to see her, he couldn't be this aggressive. He didn't know what had happened to her, but whatever it was, it wasn't good. Instinctively, he knew that Rowan had had enough truculent men in her life.

By the time the bottle emptied he had made a decision. He was going up there, and he wouldn't take no for answer. He wouldn't be combative about it or anything, but enough was enough. He was going to talk to Rowan.

Knocking quietly on her door, Shane tired to push his disquiet down. He could hear her inside moving around so he knocked again, this time harder.

"Justin, you forget your key?" Rowan asked as the door flew open.

His breath stopped when his eyes locked with hers. He had to brace himself against the doorframe, leaning on his upper arm.

"Hi," he almost whispered.

"Hi," she whispered back, still holding the door.